FREEDOM

Exhilaration surged sparkling in Cathy. For the first time in over a year she was out on her own, alone, by herself, unescorted by any other human being, restricted to the guidance of no one's arm, the whim of no one's voice. She knew how a bird must feel on discovering the door of his cage is open. She was free again, independent and whole, and it was a thousand times more glorious than she had remembered.

When they halted at the curb before their third street crossing, Cathy couldn't resist bending to give her dog a quick hug of appreciation. "Trudy, you're wonderful!"

Trudy's tail swayed briefly. Her nose lifted to touch Cathy's cheek, then switched back for a survey of the street ahead. From alert head to tip-curled tail, her pose seemed to be saying "This is just the beginning."

LIGHT
A SINGLE
CANDLE

Beverly Butler

AN ARCHWAY PAPERBACK
Published by POCKET BOOKS • NEW YORK

An Archway Paperback published by
POCKET BOOKS, a division of Simon & Schuster, Inc.
1230 Avenue of the Americas, New York, N.Y 10020

ISBN: 0-671-44385-2

First Pocket Books printing March, 1970

25 24 23 22 21 20 19

AN ARCHWAY PAPERBACK and colophon are
registered trademarks of Simon & Schuster, Inc.

Printed in the U.S.A.

IL 7+

To Sister Mary Hester, Dorothy M. Bryan,
and my father,
all of whom wanted this book

1

GRAVEL SPATTERED as Cathy spun her bike around the corner of the alley and coasted full speed toward the blackness that was the open garage door. The garage itself was a radiant white blur in the July sun, and wide though the door was, she had to screw her forehead up in a fierce squint to make the outlines come clear enough for safety as she rolled up over the ramp and into the darkness. Even after she jumped off and was pushing the front wheel into the rack that kept the bike from falling down in the way of the car, the blur still swam before her. She pulled off her glasses, breathed on them hard and rubbed them on the pocket of her cotton shirt.

Pete Sheridan's bike shrieked to a stop outside the door. Pete had never brought himself to take that turn in the alley at the speed Cathy did, but neither could she equal his ability to slam on the brakes like that without pitching headfirst over the handle bars.

"Hey, Cathy," he called, "what time are you going to be back this afternoon? Do you know?"

"No," Cathy said ruefully, "but probably too late to do anything. Those doctors take forever, especially if there's a good reason I'd rather be at home." She hooked her glasses over her ears again, and solid form returned to the objects about her. "Maybe it will be worth it, though, if they have my new glasses ready today. I can't even see to read with these any more."

"Well, it sure seems dumb to me to waste your birthday at the eye doctor's," Pete said, for his own vision was pilot perfect, and he was not inclined to stir himself far to look at things from the other fellow's point of view. "Wait until my fourteenth birthday gets here. I'll show you the real way to celebrate."

Cathy had no doubt that he would. She and Pete had been celebrating each other's birthdays since they were seven, which amounted to exactly half her life now, and she had long ago admitted that Pete's were more exciting, mainly because the Sheridans' backyard boasted a grill, tile fireplace and stone barbecue pit which were the smoky, mouth-watering center of every occasion.

Nevertheless, she would not have accepted a thousand barbecue pits in trade for this birthday today, with its stack of gifts that had awaited her at the breakfast table this morning and, most particularly, the thin, narrow box that had crowned the pile. At this moment, her only wish that remained unfulfilled was for the new glasses that would replace these she was outgrowing so rapidly.

This was not the sort of thing she could say to Pete very well, however. He was her best friend, so much so that her other friends were hardly more than acquaintances by comparison. Nobody could match him as a companion when it came to climbing trees or racing bikes or working jigsaw puzzles or building a toboggan slide or doing any of the countless activities they had invented together throughout the years. But he wasn't the storybook kind of friend you confided your most intimate hopes and ponderings to, because he wouldn't listen, or if he did, he would laugh rather than try to understand.

So, as she walked out onto the ramp and pulled on the rope to bring down the overhead door, she said merely, "If you weren't leaving for your summer cottage as soon as your dad gets home from work tonight, you'd see plenty of celebration at my house, anyway. I don't leave town on your birthdays."

"You can't. My birthday's in October, and you have to stick around for school." He braced himself on one tiptoe, his right foot planted on the raised pedal, readying himself for a quick take-off. "Call me if you get back early enough to do anything. Otherwise, so long for a few weeks."

"O.K.," Cathy said. "So long."

He grunted, shoved his foot against the pedal and rolled off down the alley without a backward look.

Cathy did not believe in backward looks either, once good-bys were said, but she watched him until he was beyond his own garage, three doors from hers. These next few weeks promised to be pretty dull while he was gone. Not that she didn't know of plenty of kids from school, if she wanted to hunt them up, but they all had their special friends, too, and she spent so little time among them when Pete was around that she always felt somewhat like an outsider. Still, the pang of loneliness she usually felt at the prospect of the Sheridans' summer vacation did not pinch her quite so sharply today. There was that beautiful, thin box of hers to think of instead.

She ran up the terrace steps—and nearly fell headlong over the hose her brother Mark was using to fill a tub for wading.

"Pick up your feet, clumsy," Mark said ungraciously.

When she made a gesture toward wresting the nozzle from his grasp—a skirmish in which her six years' advantage of age and size would inevitably decide the result—he added hastily, "You better get your clothes changed in a hurry. Daddy called already to say that he's starting home from the office to take you to your appointment So run."

He punctuated this advice by suddenly aiming the hose at her feet. Cathy sensed rather than saw the stream of water coming and jumped aside in time to save all but the heel of one sneaker from a wetting. It was an ideal excuse for a battle, but her mother's voice, descending on them from an upstairs window, ended the war at its start.

"Cathy, you have just fifteen minutes to get washed and dressed. If you aren't ready when your father gets here, you'll have to do the explaining."

Cathy did not need to be told twice. If there was one thing her father insisted on, it was that everyone be punctual, even early, for appointments, and she did not want to inflict any lectures on herself on her birthday. Besides, if there should be a chance that she could have the new glasses to put on the minute she arrived so she could be home again with hours to spare before Pete left, she did not want to spoil it.

She sprinted across the yard, kicked off her sneakers in the back hall and raced in stocking feet through the kitchen and up the stairs to her room. Her blue dress, a crisp white slip and a clean pair of socks were lying on the bed for her, and she began peeling off her blue jeans as soon as she crossed the threshold. Just inside the door, however, glistening on top of the dresser, lay the narrow, black box, her birthday box. She could not resist pausing to lift the lid and finger the two dozen smooth, softly colored cylinders it protected. They were pastels, genuine professional artist's chalks, the biggest step yet along the road to achieving her heart's desire, that of some day becoming a great artist, almost as great, perhaps, as Rembrandt or Leonardo da Vinci. She had no recollection of when this ambition had first taken root within her; it seemed always to have been a part of her, surviving unshaken and unshakeable through even her most violent grade school enthusiasms for the careers of nursing, being a stewardess on international flights, or of digging up archaeological wonders under the white-hot sun of Egypt.

"I thought as much," her mother said as she entered the room, putting on an air of exaggerated sternness. "You get yourself dressed, young lady, and in a hurry, or I'll put a padlock on that box. If it's so vital that those chalks be looked at every hour on the hour, why didn't you carry them with you this morning, like Pete was urging you to?"

"I was afraid they'd get broken, bouncing around in a bike basket," Cathy answered. Reluctantly and lovingly, she lowered the lid, and set to work unbuttoning her shirt. "Besides, we weren't sure where we were going to eat our picnic until we were practically there, and I don't want to use them up making pictures of just any old thing."

Her mother held the slip up for her, spreading its

skirt in preparation for dropping it down over Cathy's head. "How was the picnic?"

"Fine." Arms flailing in search of the shoulder straps, Cathy dove upward through the folds of crisp white cotton. While her face was muffled and hidden, she enlarged carelessly, "We ate at Ridge Park."

"All the way to Ridge Park? Cathy, you didn't!" Her mother withdrew a step to eye her from head to toe, as though she did not trust the evidence of her ears alone. "Your father and I both told you to stay off those busy streets with your bike until you have a pair of glasses strong enough to let you see what you are doing."

"There wasn't too much traffic," Cathy said, but more for appearance's sake than because she felt she had any adequate grounds of defense. To tell the truth, it was not a journey she would willingly venture on again without sharper vision, no matter how scornful or insistent Pete was—but the results of this morning's ride had proved well worth the risk.

It was nearly as great a risk, perhaps, to continue the discussion now, instead of following the course of true wisdom, which would be to try and change the subject, but she was too elated by her discovery to keep it to herself any longer. "We climbed that trail that goes up through the woods, the one you have to walk single file on, to find out where it ends," she explained, sitting flat on the floor to don the fresh socks and buckle her white sandals. "We didn't find out, though, because it was too far and I had to get home, but I did find the scene I'm going to do for my first picture with my chalks. It's a little clearing in the woods, right at the edge of the bluff, so that it's full of sunlight and tree shadows, and you can see the lake right in front of you. It looks just like the sky starts where the bluff stops. It's beautiful."

"It does sound like a lovely picture," her mother agreed, but, as Cathy's better judgment had foreseen, no amount of beauty the park could offer was sufficient to lure attention from the fact that the park was some three miles distant and on the wrong side of several major streets carrying heavy cross-town traffic. "Unless you're not planning to use those pastels right away, though," her mother went on, "you might as well hunt around for a scene nearer to home for your first picture. I'm not going to let you cruise the town like that until I'm positive you can take care of yourself, and you may be sure your father will second me."

Cathy opened her mouth to object, but shut it again, deciding to listen without interruption so that the lecture would be done sooner. Out of consideration for her birthday, it was milder than she had expected, but the knowledge that every word of it was deserved was of no comfort.

It did have the happy effect of hurrying her, however—an effect which few methods of direct prodding could boast of producing. She did not even dawdle over combing her short hair, as she usually did, squinting into the mirror to see if it were showing any signs yet of darkening to the glowing auburn of her mother's. Everyone, aunts, grandparents and friends, kept predicting that some day it most surely would, but, thus far, her crowning glory flaunted the brightness of carrots well scrubbed. Anyway, it was probably no darker than it had been this morning, when she had inspected it with extra thoroughness in the half-serious hope that her new age might make itself evident in one way or another.

A full five minutes before Mark banged in through the back door to yell that the car was on its way down the street, she was rotating with clean face, smooth hair and crisp, summer-blue dress, neatly buttoned, in front of her mother for examination and approval.

"Slick as a whistle," her mother nodded, smiling approvingly, "trim as a biscuit and pretty as a picture." She bent to straighten a tilted-up section of hem, then stood a little farther off for a second view. "They say clothes don't make the man, but there must be a different rule for girls. I don't know how else to explain the transformation of such a tomboy into a young lady in just ten minutes."

Cathy grinned and gave her starchy skirts an airy swirl. She liked the idea of being able to become a young lady at will—that is, if she didn't have to stick to the character too long and could rely on her blue jeans and sneakers always staying within reasonable reach. The brightness of her birthday mood floated around her again like the perfume of the climbing roses drifting in through the open windows as she ran downstairs.

"Here he is! Daddy's here!" Mark announced, shouting the news in at the front screen this time. He galloped on to greet the car, leaving a trail of wet, brown footprints on the white walk.

Cathy, grown a trifle more mindful of her dignity, accepted the handkerchief her mother thrust into her hand and proceeded to the car at as rapid a pace as she felt was compatible with the stature of a young lady freshly arrived at the age of fourteen.

Mark, already standing within the opened car door, although forbidden to seat himself because of his dripping swimming trunks, destroyed the illusion for her by inquiring, "What you walking stiff-legged for? Your shoes pinch?"

Cathy ignored him completely, except to think how pleasant it would be if her shoe should happen by accident to land firmly on his bare toes, but he had the presence of mind and the nimbleness to remove himself and his toes to the other side of the door before she was in pressing range. She wondered, as she had wondered on occasions beyond number, why, if it were necessary that she have a younger brother, it could not have been one like Pete Sheridan. This was a question she generally kept to herself, however, not only because her parents did not share her low opinion of Mark, but also because they did not altogether share her high regard for Pete. It was, she felt, simply the faculty most adults had of looking at things from too wide an angle and basing their judgment on points that were scarcely related to the immediate problem at all.

Her father stretched an arm in front of her to wave at the house. Cathy leaned out to wave, too, guessing that her mother was standing in the doorway, although she could distinguish nothing but the long rectangle of the screen door, dark against the creamy stone of the house.

"Good-by, Mom," she called as the motor rumbled into action. Then, leaning out farther, she cooed in a super-sweet tone, "Bye, bye, Markie. Be good."

The car slid away from the curb, and Mark, in his red trunks, was left behind, helpless to seek revenge for either the advice or the despised name. Cathy settled herself comfortably on the seat to watch in contentment the endless glide of sun-flecked tree shadows over the dusty green hood of the engine.

"Well, how is the birthday progressing?" her father asked, glancing down at her.

"Perfect so far." She tipped her face to catch the warm July breeze and the smell of sprinkler-wet lawns. There was nothing dishonest about choosing to postpone an account of the Ridge Park incident until later, particularly when she had more pressing matters to consider now. "It will be all perfect if Dr. Kruger has my glasses ready. I'll have to save my pastels forever if I don't get rid of these old ones, because they show me hardly anything any more. Do you think Dr. Kruger might have the new ones by today?"

"I don't know," her father said. "This is a special appointment he made for you himself, so there must be something in the wind."

Cathy thought that never before in her life had glasses taken such an eternity to be replaced, and she had been wearing them since she was five. They were barely less a part of her than her teeth, and normally she gave them about the same amount of thought. Every year or two, she had gone to have her eyes tested, and, within a few days, she would have a new pair of glasses adjusted to her changing size and needs. It had been no more complicated than that.

But this spring, when she went for her check-up, gray-haired Dr. Stirling was gone, retired to Florida to live near his grandchildren. In his place was young Dr. Kruger, fresh from his hitch in the Navy and full of strange methods and ideas that seemed to drag on forever without accomplishing a thing. He would press two fingers on top of first one, then the other of her eyes while he had her look at the floor. He sat her at an impressive apparatus that had a cup to hold her chin and a brace to steady her forehead against, and while she stared in at one end of the instrument, he went around and stared at her through the other. He put numbing drops in her eyes and had her lie on a table, both eyes wide open, while he set another kind of instrument right on their surface. None of this hurt her, nor, after she went through it once, did it scare her at all. But it happened appointment after appointment after appointment, gobbling the best portions of Saturday afternoons during the school year and, now that vacation was here, seeking out special days like this to bite into.

Dr. Kruger was a silent young man, who did not smile if there were any other expression he could possibly substitute. He was very gentle about everything he did, but it never occurred to him to explain what he was doing or why. Cathy could not recall his ever speaking a word to her that was not a direction of some sort: "Come this way, Cathy." "Don't move your eyes, Cathy." "Look straight ahead and try not to blink." She had the disquieting impression sometimes that she was just an interesting specimen to him, no more intelligent or human than the garden bugs she and Pete studied through a magnifying glass. It was fun to speculate on how he might leap up in horrified astonishment if she should suddenly compliment him on his tie or ask him where he got the stuffed fish hanging on his waiting room wall, but his gravity was too awing for her really to dare such a thing. Worse than anything else, though, was the unpleasant fact that she was outgrowing her old glasses faster every day. She could no longer focus sharply enough to read print smaller than headlines. Yet Dr. Kruger appeared to have entirely forgotten about her need for new glasses. If only he would re-

11

member and give them to her, she knew she could forgive him everything.

Her father drove into the parking lot opposite the tall, downtown office building that housed Dr. Kruger in one corner of its highest floor. They took a stomach-twirling upward rush in an elevator and entered the doctor's carpeted waiting room.

"Good afternoon, Mr. Wheeler and Cathy," the nurse at the desk greeted them. She had a pretty smile and a happy voice, but if she had a name, no one in the office ever spoke it, at least, not within Cathy's hearing. "You're right on the dot for your appointment. Wonderful! And for once, Dr. Kruger is ready for you right away. I'll call him."

Cathy's heart jumped. This was something out of the ordinary. She glanced up at her father, hoping he would comment, but Dr. Kruger was already striding toward them from his inner office. With him was another man, short, plump and rather pink in contrast to Dr. Kruger's tall, lean darkness.

"Mr. Wheeler," Dr. Kruger said, "this is Dr. Jameson of the University Clinic. I've mentioned him to you before. When I learned he was going to be in town this week, I asked him to stop by here and have a look at Cathy."

The men shook hands. Then, to Cathy's surprise, Dr. Jameson extended his right hand toward her. "Hello, Cathy," he said, his stubby, thick fingers swallowing hers in a warm squeeze. "You may not believe this, but I've been doing a considerable amount of reading about you today. You and I are practically old friends. What do you say we go back in that machine shop Dr. Kruger calls his lab and get better acquainted?"

Cathy was so used to being ignored in the presence

of Dr. Kruger that, for the moment, she could think of nothing to say. Dr. Jameson spared her the trouble by pouring forth a running flow of lively chatter himself as he led her into the familiar room of tables and instruments and seated her in the big, leather, dentist-type chair that was always allotted to her.

His idea of getting better acquainted was to do the same eye-pressing, light-flashing tests on her that Dr. Kruger did each time, but she hardly noticed them for giggling at the ridiculous jokes he insisted on telling the whole while. Besides, he did not deliberate over each test or repeat it as Dr. Kruger did, but performed them briskly and confidently, as though he knew in advance what they would show. What really won her heart, though, was his decision to skip the test she disliked most, and to substitute the reading chart instead.

"It's no fun lying still on a table on a nice summer afternoon," he said, as if he thought maybe he owed her an apology, "and they tell me those eye drops sting a bit. I wouldn't want to sting such pretty blue eyes as yours if I didn't have to. Let's see how good you are at reading gibberish with them."

Cathy beamed at him, almost forgetting her awe of Dr. Kruger's office in her eagerness to skirt the table and line herself up with the screen on which a machine projected the letters of the chart. This was the test that always came before she got new glasses, and the one test Dr. Kruger hadn't bothered to give her since the first time she was here. She hoped he was watching and listening and taking notes on how a real doctor handled things.

Maybe some of her hope was a little too obvious in her expression, for, when she finished reading the few lines of the chart that she could make out, even by

13

guessing, Dr. Jameson patted her on the shoulder and said, "I bet Dr. Kruger never told you he went to school under me a few years ago and was my best student. You wouldn't think that of a shy fellow like him, would you? But these quiet fellows have plenty of good stuff inside, sometimes, and anything Bob Kruger tells you to do, you can be sure it's the best thing to be done." He turned her toward the big dentist chair and handed her her glasses, which had managed to disappear during the testings. "Why don't you curl up here and wait in style until your dad is set to take you home?" he suggested.

Cathy climbed obediently into the chair and settled herself to be patient while the two doctors went off to speak to her father. She wished they would hurry, but she had enough to think about if they did not—too much, in fact. She pushed the revelation about Dr. Kruger into a side pocket of her mind, to be examined more thoroughly another time. Who would ever have suspected that he was shy? That any grownups were, for that matter, and especially a person as important as a doctor?

But excitement was twirling in her like the stripes of a candy cane, and it had nothing to do with the personality of Dr. Kruger. She swung her left foot to and fro over the edge of the chair, letting her sandal heel bump the chair and bounce forward and her toe bump the foot rest that was too low for her and bounce back. Surely everything that had happened this afternoon pointed to her finally having her new glasses. If they were not ready for her today, they would be in a day or two. Probably that was what the doctors were talking to her father about, telling where and when he could get them for her. And once she had them—!

14

She sucked in her lower lip, imagining the Ridge Park clearing as she had seen it this morning, all green and golden and blue, and as it would be done in the soft, warm shadings of pastels. How did artists achieve the effect of sunlight flooding a scene, she wondered. Perhaps she should go to the library first and study a book of reproductions. Rembrandt and Van Gogh might be the best for a start . . .

Her foot slowed its swinging, and she sat motionless for a minute, lost in plans for tomorrow. The voices of her father and the doctors talking not far beyond the door, hummed like bees in the background of her daydream. Then, for no reason, she became aware of the discussion, and Dr. Kruger's drawl, mild but penetrating, slid without warning into her consciousness:

"I'd advise having her learn to read Braille as soon as possible."

Braille! Cathy's breath went from her as though she were hit in the stomach. The walls around her quivered like words in italics, and shrank in on her. She could get no air. It was too compressed within the shrunken room, too hot and thick to drag into her lungs. A funnel of dizziness spun darkness about her. She clutched the wide, black arm of the chair and dropped her head onto it, to avoid being sucked off.

Where the nurse appeared from, she had no idea, but there she was, helping her to sit up and offering her a paper cup of icy water. Cathy sipped automatically, and the weight faded from her lungs, the walls retreated to their proper distance.

But she did not want more water. She did not want the windows opened to their utmost, as Dr. Kruger was doing. She did not want to answer the nurse's worried questions. She did not want to have her spirits lifted by Dr. Jameson's heartiness as he and her father came to stand over her.

"I want to go home," she said, ignoring everyone but her father as completely as ever Dr. Kruger had ignored her. She did not care if she sounded rude or childish. She was too desperate to remember even that such a likelihood existed. "Daddy, let's go!"

None of them tried to argue her into resting longer or insisted on delaying for some other reason, as she was half afraid they would. What it was they did say to her, however, was lost in a mist of confusion that was rising between her and the outside world, like a protective smoke cloud. Nothing registered definitely on her senses until she was somehow beside her father in the car, its motor throbbing to join the busy stream of traffic.

"Feeling better?" her father asked. He touched the back of his hand to her forehead and appeared satisfied. "What happened? An overdose of picnic lunch?"

"No." But as she said it, an uneasiness stirred in her stomach, urging that he might be right. Maybe she was sick. Maybe everything else was a piece of soured imagination because she was sick from the heat or the picnic.

"You're sure you're all right?" her father persisted.

She nodded—and knew it was not her stomach that was wrong, for the uneasiness hardened to a knot that was thrusting itself up through her chest toward her throat to choke her. "Let's go home, please."

He asked her no more, but, as the car moved along the crowded streets, he cast an anxious glance sideways at her from time to time.

Cathy uncurled her damp palms to the breeze from the window. She wanted to tell him what was wrong, she was aching to tell him, but to put the thing into words, to say it aloud— Her tongue was dry, and she wished she had swallowed more of the water in the paper cup.

Twice her lips parted to frame the doctor's name, but twice her throat refused to let any sound escape. The rows of dingy office buildings, glass-fronted stores and downtown apartments were yielding to the grassy lawns and tree-lined avenues of the suburbs when the words finally burst out by themselves: "He said I should learn Braille!"

Her father shot another keen glance at her, then fixed his gaze straight ahead on the road. "Yes," he said calmly. "he thinks you should learn Braille."

"But Braille is for blind people!" she cried, and the whole of the terrible thing was spoken.

Her father's tanned face swerved not an inch from his scrutiny of the road. "It's for anybody who can't see well enough to read print." He paused for a moment, then continued. "Dr. Jameson is one of the best eye specialists there is, and Dr. Kruger's reputation as an oculist is getting to be just about as good, but there are certain kinds of damage to eyes that the very best doctor on earth can't repair. All that can be done is to prevent the damage from going further."

"What kind of damage?" Cathy asked, in such a small voice she wondered that he heard her.

"They call it glaucoma. It means that the pressure in your eyes is building up higher and higher because the tiny drainage canals that should take care of it are blocked or too little. The pressure kills the optic nerve, bit by bit. What's dead can't be brought to life again, but there is hope that the living part can be saved.

Dr. Jameson thinks you ought to have an operation right away."

Cathy bent her head, fighting down the knot that was swelling in her chest to where there was barely space for her heart to beat. Her father was treating her like a grownup, talking as though he was sure she was capable of understanding the facts and accepting them. She liked it when he did that. She couldn't risk showing him how ungrownup and scared she really felt.

"What if the operation doesn't work?"

"Operations practically always work nowadays. It will be over in less than two weeks from today, and you'll finally have your new glasses. If they can't do as well as the old ones used to, at least you'll have as much vision as you do now. Maybe you could even read print with a magnifying glass. That won't be so bad, will it?"

"No," Cathy managed to answer. She found it helped to stare straight ahead, as he did, to gaze at the thick green of the trees, the dull gray of the pavement and its wriggling veins of black tar, the yellow dots of dandelions spotting the lawns. A boy in red trunks like Mark's and a girl in a pink sun suit were running through the sprinkler in one yard. The entire sidewalk in front of their house was wet and glistening. It looked like a stick of fresh chewing gum after its dust of sugar was licked off. The sky was water pale and immensely distant, and in it were puffy clouds like gobs of suds from a detergent. How would it be if she were unable to see any of this ever again.

A twitch of her legs, a stiffening of her knees, drove the notion from her. She had her father's word that matters would never be that bad.

Yet, when he halted to let her out at the front walk

before he took the car on around to the alley and the garage, she flew across the yard to the shelter of the house as though a monster were pursuing her.

Her mother, mending a shirt of Mark's by the light of the living-room window, half rose to meet her. "Cathy, what's wrong?"

Cathy hesitated, then ran to her. The need to preserve her dignity, the need to be reasonable and brave was gone. She was home at last, safe where no strangers could see, no terrors could touch her. Crumpling to her knees, she buried her face in her mother's lap and sobbed until the knot of panic in her melted and was washed away.

2

IT WAS ARRANGED that the operation should take place exactly one week to the day after Cathy's visit to Dr. Kruger's office. During the time between, she didn't talk about it much, and neither did her parents, at least not in her hearing, but it was much harder not to think about it, especially when she woke up in the morning and just before she fell asleep at night. It was like the high slide at the Ridge Park swimming beach: once you had climbed to the top of it, you were committed to letting yourself go, and, no matter what else you thought of as you hurtled downward, you knew the water was there at the end, cold and deep and sooner than you wanted it. She was almost relieved when the day she was to leave for the hospital finally did arrive.

"Tom Schultz went to the hospital the week school was out this summer," Mark said from a perch astride the steel frame of the back yard swing while he and Cathy were idling away her last half hour at home. "All he had to eat was ice cream, as much as he could hold."

"That's because he had his tonsils out," Cathy said.

She hooked her elbows around the ropes and sagged forward in the swing, watching the lazy advance and retreat of the dusty, worn patch in the grass directly under her feet. "Ice cream is good for sore throats because it's easy to swallow. I'll probably get just ordinary food, the same as I did when I had my appendix out."

"I remember that!" Mark banged his heels against the frame. "I was only six years old then, and I couldn't come in the hospital to see you because I was too healthy and might have germs. They don't mind the germs on sick kids, though. It's not fair. I'm eight years old, and nobody's let me have a look inside a hospital since I was born."

Cathy slapped her feet flat to the ground, bringing the swing to an impatient halt. "Don't you ever talk sense?" She gave the earth a push with her toes, and began to pump once more, her mood of sun-soaked detachment ruined.

"Can't talk sense to people who can't understand," Mark said philosophically. He extended a leg above her to block the nearest rope and pitch her sideways, but changed his mind when it appeared the rough hemp was also about to saw a path across his ankle. "Hey, Cathy? Will your operation hurt, do you think? Are you scared?"

She tossed her head and pumped harder, to outrace a tiny ripple of chill down her back. "Don't be dumb. They put you to sleep when they operate. I spent a week in the hospital two years ago, and I wasn't scared then, was I? So what makes you think I'd be scared now?" Before he could answer, she jumped free of the swing on its forward rise and marched into the house, leaving him to follow or stay aloft as he pleased.

For her own sake as much as for his education, she

21

had to keep on being scornfully independent, even after her mother called them to the car and the journey to the hospital was actually under way. When he and his suitcase were deposited on the curb in front of Grandma Wheeler's, where he was to spend the night, she had an odd feeling that she would have liked to have been nicer to him—and perhaps more honest with everyone. But it was too late to do anything for Mark except wave and smile as she drove off, and too late to consider any last-minute confessions because the last minute, in the shape of the huge, red-brick hospital, was looming in her path by almost the very next breath, it seemed.

She wished, a little ashamed of herself, that she were young enough to cling to her mother's hand going in through the big doors and up to the reception desk. But, once there, listening to her father give the receptionist the information about name, age, doctors and so on that was necessary for admittance, she realized that she wasn't as scared as she expected she would be. In fact, she was hardly scared at all. Although this was not the same hospital she had been in two years ago, she began to recognize a sameness in the routine of acceptance that was most comforting. There was the X-ray of her chest, the finger-pricking blood test that reminded her of *Tom Sawyer,* the ride upstairs in an elevator smelling of antiseptics, and the nurse—a young, curly-haired nurse with a happy giggle—who shooed her parents out of the room and helped her undress. There was also the intern in a white coat, who came in to listen to her heart and hit her on the back and knees with a rubber hammer.

"I guess you can count on being around a number of years," he said, grinning. "You'll be escaping from us in no time, just like all the other redheads we try to capture."

Cathy laughed, sitting cross-legged in the middle of the lofty white bed—but soon she was wondering if it was as much of a joke as she thought. Time was slipping away from her at the rate of hours in the space of minutes, its support vanishing from under her like the last few inches on the water slide. Her parents were hardly seated in the chairs beside her bed when her supper arrived on a tray. Her stomach, for some reason, rebelled at the sight of food, refusing to harbor more than a swallow from each dish, yet scarcely had she finished that much when the rattle of carts in the hall signaled the trays were being gathered up. Then evening visitors were thronging the halls, passing by the door, creating a busy murmur in the air, and the next thing she knew, a loud-speaker was announcing the end of visiting hours.

Her father stood up. "I suppose that we should go, too." He squeezed her hand. "Behave yourself and get a good night's sleep. We'll see you tomorrow."

Cathy moved her lips in a smile, but held tight to his hand. This was the worst moment of all. "Will you be here before they take me to the operating room? It'll be early, eight o'clock."

"We'll be here," he promised firmly, drawing his hand free.

"Of course, we will." Her mother kissed her and smoothed the rumpled sheet. "Don't worry now. Everything's going to be fine. By this time tomorrow night, it will all be over."

There was nothing Cathy could do but nod and watch them disappear through the door. The black hands of her father's traveling clock, ticking on the bedside stand, suddenly checked their hurry, and seemed to come to a standstill. This time tomorrow was a thousand years off, and likely to stay there.

"Kind of quiet in here, isn't it?" a voice broke in on her pensiveness, and the nurse with the giggle walked in. "The trouble is, hospitals aren't as quiet as people think. Most people can't rest their first night here because of the activity going on in the halls, so we usually give everyone a little pill like this to help them relax."

Cathy didn't feel that she was going to sleep much, either, but it wasn't because of the noise in the corridors. She did not believe that even a pill would be of any great help, especially one as tiny as the pellet in the paper cup the nurse was offering her, but she gulped it down. It was an excuse for drinking through the bent glass tube in her water glass, anyway, which was rather fun.

"Fine," the nurse approved. "I can tell you're going to be one of my favorite patients. I practically have to wrestle with some of the people we get in here to make them take what they should." She giggled, punching the pillow into shape. "Naturally, those are the folks who stay the longest, too. Why don't you lie back and take it easy for a while, and I'll be in again later to see how you're doing."

But later never came—at least as far as her patient was aware. Cathy lay back to please her, closing her eyes for "only a second" . . . but when she opened them, a different nurse was at her bed, and daylight was pouring in at the windows.

Everything after that happened in rapid sequence. Cathy's temperature was taken. A flabby rubber hose wrapped around her arm and inflated, to check her blood pressure. A hypodermic needle was jabbed in her other arm, while she set her teeth and pretended not to notice the sting. Finally, she had to shed her blue-striped pajamas and let the nurse tie her into a smock-like hospital gown that reached to her knees and didn't quite meet behind.

The hands of the traveling clock were leaping ahead now; seven-thirty, seven-forty, quarter to eight. Cathy was growing rather lightheaded, the effect of the hypo, she supposed, as she tried to fix the details of how it felt in her memory so she could report to Pete. But, in spite of that, tiny coils of anxiety were tightening her nerves at every minute that passed without bringing her parents. She didn't know just how anxious she was, though, until, at ten minutes of eight, they walked in, and she heard the relief in her own voice as she exclaimed, "You made it!"

"Why, Cathy," her mother said, the sympathy in her voice as warm as the fingers she pressed against her daughter's cheek. "You weren't afraid we wouldn't, were you? I thought you knew better than that."

Her father came to the other side of the bed. "We won't desert you. We were delayed because we met Dr. Kruger downstairs. He says to tell you not to worry."

There was no chance to talk more, for the nurse was wheeling in the long, narrow cart that was to carry Cathy to wherever it was that Dr. Kruger was waiting. It was a comfortable cart, and Cathy was glad to stretch out on it. Perhaps it was the giddiness, but she wasn't worried any more.

She did not remember if she said good-by as the rubber-tired wheels rolled smoothly away with her, but she did remember how her parents looked, standing at the foot of the bed when she left. Sunlight bathed them both, turning her mother's hair to dark, rich fire above the cool green of her dress, and accenting the square set of her father's shoulders, the vividness of his summer tan in contrast to his gray suit and white shirt.

The walls of the operating room were green, too, but paler than her mother's dress, a subdued, restful kind of green, the color Cathy imagined sea water must be. Lying flat as she was, and with the world becoming somewhat wavering and unreal, the cool walls and an impression of large windows were as much of the room as she could observe. Her body felt almost too heavy to lift as someone helped her slide from the cart to the white operating table, yet she had an oddly pleasant sensation of being about to float off unless they strapped her down. Dr. Kruger, grave and calm as though he were in his office, spoke to her from an angle of the room she could not see. He said good morning and asked her if everything was going all right. Before she could answer, her nose and the lower part of her face were covered by something chill and wet.

"Breathe deeply, Cathy," said someone. "Count to a hundred aloud . . . and breathe deeply."

A smell like fingernail polish, only sweeter, filled her nose. She didn't like it, but she knew it was ether and that the sooner it put her to sleep, the sooner she would be unaware of the smell.

"One," she began, breathing in quickly and exhaling the words, "two, three, four, five . . ."

The numbers echoed in her head. They boomed and faded and boomed, like reverberations in a cave. She heard *five* repeating, repeating, repeating, until it was lost in remoteness . . . And the water at the end of the slide closed above her.

When Cathy struggled up to the surface once more, she was in bed. Her mother was holding her hand and talking to her, telling her the operation was over and she was safe, telling her not to touch the bandages on her eyes.

Cathy did touch them, but later, during the night, when no one was near, and gently, just to find out what sort of bandages they were. At first, she was tempted to peep out from underneath if she could, but there were strips of adhesive crisscrossed everywhere, with a padding of cotton and gauze beneath and a blindfold affair tied across the top and stuck in place with more tape, so she decided it was easier—as well as wiser—not to meddle.

Besides, although her eyes were in no pain, they were surprisingly weak from their ordeal. The slightest turn of her head sent tears flooding to wet the gauze as though she were crying, and the very thought of light had the same watery effect as staring too long at the sun or into the wind. It was worse when Dr. Kruger came in the morning to change the dressings. Her eyelids screwed shut of themselves so fiercely that he had to pry them open with his fingers, and then the tiny slit he achieved was not large enough for any light to reach her through the flow of tears it created. She did her best to cooperate, but it was the same battle every day, and always the eyelids won their fight for darkness.

Or so Cathy thought until, on her last morning at the hospital, Dr. Kruger climaxed the daily trial of strength by saying, "Now, Cathy, I want you to look straight up and tell me exactly what you see."

She dug the back of her head deeper into the pillow, to brace herself for the effort. His thumb and finger were firm against her face above and below her eye, but her own hands flew to do the opening of the lids herself. Instead, her fingers encountered the waxy curve of lashes raised to where they almost brushed her eyebrow. The lower lashes were a stiff fringe at the top of her cheek bone. Her eye was wide open already.

"Look hard," Dr. Kruger said. "Do you see the light?"

She did look hard, the hardest she had ever looked in her life. What she saw was blackness, thinned here and there to dark red-brown. At the edges of these thin spots, pin pricks of white light showed through. It reminded her of the old Christmas tree lights in the attic, which had their color painted on the outside of the glass and shone white wherever specks of the paint were chipped off or cracked.

"I see speckles," she said. "That's all."

He released her eyelids without comment and transferred his fingers to the other eye. A few larger flecks of light penetrated the blackness there, but they were mostly a dingy yellow tinge, like old plastic. And they were only flecks in blackness.

Cathy didn't ask him why, or what it meant; she didn't want to ask him. She wasn't sure she wanted to ask anyone. She simply wanted her mother and her father—yes, and Mark, even Mark—wanted them so suddenly and so sharply that her heart nearly burst before Dr. Kruger finally left and she could ease the misery by burying her face in the pillow while the new bandages grew sodden—for once with hot, genuine tears.

There were no more tears to cry by the time Cathy heard her mother's voice in the corridor, but the excitement of knowing she was about to go home was dried up, too. She lay still, her fists knobs of wood under the pillow, her whole body rigid, almost as though she were afraid to move.

"Cathy?" her mother said from the door. Her quick step, lighter than the following tread of Cathy's father, tapped across the space of tile floor to the bedside. "Cathy, are you sleeping?"

Cathy rolled her head from side to side to signify no. Then, in a whisper that seemed nevertheless to shatter the air, she breathed the only words that were in her mind: "I can't see."

For a moment, absolute silence filled the room. Bewildered, she turned on her side, facing where she thought they ought to be. "Mom? Daddy?" Her hand, groping in search of them, was caught and pressed by two, one of them slim and warm, the other stronger and broader.

"We're right here," her mother said. "It's just that Dr. Kruger told us he didn't think you realized—"

"That proves how good Dr. Kruger's thinking is," Cathy said in a surge of bitterness that was entirely new to her. "He thought I needed an operation instead of glasses, too. He thought we were lucky to get into the hospital this soon. He thought nothing could go wrong. He thought everything would be fine. He thinks a lot of things!"

She tried to wrench her hand free and fling herself on her face again, but her father's grip tightened, keeping her prisoner. "Cathy, stop that," he said, but his tone was merely grave, not angry. "You should know that, if we believed there was a better doctor for this operation, your mother and I would have had him for you at any price. You should also know that, if we believed Dr. Kruger was at fault here, we would have another doctor treating you immediately. There's a risk

29

of complications with every operation, even a cut finger, although in most cases they don't happen. But we explained to you from the beginning that, without this operation, you were bound to lose your sight in a short while, and if it went that way, there would be no chance of its ever coming back."

"Is there a chance it will come back this way?" Cathy asked quickly . . . and her heart paused between beats, waiting for the answer.

"As I understand it, some of the blood vessels in your eyes were weak, and they've burst. It's little clots of blood that are blocking the light from getting through to you. When they dissolve and disappear, there's no reason you shouldn't be able to see as well as you did before the operation. The thing is, it's not a process that will take place overnight. It needs time, and you'll have to be patient."

Cathy rubbed her heel on a wrinkle in the bed sheet, impatient already, but a smile was insisting on pulling at the muscles of her cheeks. "How much time will it need?"

"That's what nobody can say for sure." The bed creaked as her mother sat on it beside her. "It may be several weeks, or maybe several months. We'll just have to wait and see."

Wait and see. It was indefinite, but the kind of indefiniteness that preceded the surprises of a birthday or the thrills of Christmas. And when the waiting was done, she *would* see! Viewed from that angle, the waiting itself might be rather an adventure, providing no more of it had to be done in a hospital.

Cathy gave a tug at the cord pinned near the head of the bed and pressed the signal. "The nurse told me to call her when you were ready to take me home."

She grinned, her spirits rising like bubbles in ginger ale. "I've been ready for a week."

Her excitement mounted with the novelty of being trundled along the corridors of the hospital in a wheel chair and stowed away in her slippers and pajamas, amidst pillows and quilts, on the back seat of the family car. She felt herself a lady sultan, reclining at her ease in such luxury and inhaling the aromas brought her by the hot August breeze through the window. Her sense of adventure quickened as she discovered how easy it was to identify each odor and link it to the sounds that were also pouring in on her—the smell of gasoline and the ping of a filling station pump, the oily musk of the downtown river and the peculiar singing of the car's tires on the bridge, the whir of a hand lawn mower and the sweet smell of newly cut grass, the roar of a bus starting up and the kerosene smell of a diesel engine. Unbidden, a picture, complete in color and dimension, presented itself to her mind's eye to fit every noise and odor until, presently, she might almost have forgotten she was not really seeing them if it were not for the itchy adhesive on her forehead and cheeks constantly reminding her.

Arrived home, she found her role of lady sultan expanding to heights she had never imagined. For the sake of convenience, she was put into the downstairs bedroom. which otherwise belonged to Mark. and her mother's silver bell, a guarded keepsake of her wedding presents. was placed on the bedside table, to summon whatever aid Cathy would require. Mark's portable record player was on the table, too, and, beside it, a record of *The Grand Canyon Suite,* a gift from her grandmother Wheeler. And, to top things off, there was

31

her favorite dessert for lunch, ice cream, and her ultra favorite, strawberry shortcake, for dinner.

During the next few days, neighbors and well-wishers were continually dropping by to visit Cathy, and none of them came without a present of some sort to cheer her on the road to recovery. In the afternoons, her mother read aloud to her, and her father took his turn at it in the evenings. The slightest tinkle of her bell brought Mark bounding in to ask what he could do for her. One morning, he even gave her a bag of big, sweet, black cherries, bought out of his own allowance. Nothing she wanted was long in forthcoming, if it were the least bit available, and nothing she did was wrong. No one as much as commented when she played the "Cloudburst" section of her new album five times in a row at full volume, to get the effect of actual thunder.

The only drawback to this life of luxury and power was Dr. Kruger's orders that she stay flat in bed, except for an hour in the morning and another in the early evening, when she was permitted to sit quietly in a chair. Her mother let her come into the living room and lie on the davenport in the afternoon, but that quickly became as boring as being in bed. She was used to spending the summer out of doors, and the bandages on her eyes—no longer a heavy blindfold but light, gauze pads—had no effect on the locked-in energy of her arms and legs. The more restless she grew, the less there was to amuse her, and, by the end of the week, her main occupation was only to think up extra errands that the jingle of the bell would send Mark off to perform for her.

Her brother bore this with great patience, but, on the second Monday she was home, he challenged Dr. Kruger from the bedroom door, "Hey, can't she ever get up again?"

As usual, Dr. Kruger gave no indication that he heard, but, at the close of his brief examination, he said, "Well, Cathy, I guess if you are tired of beds, there is no reason why you shouldn't get up and stay up, starting tomorrow. We'll leave those bandages on for another couple of days, though, just for luck."

Under other circumstances, Mark's yelp of joy would have roused her indignation to its fullest, but she was too elated herself to mind that he was celebrating his freedom more than hers. The truth was, she could have hugged him.

"You needn't stick around here this morning while Mom's in the basement, washing," she told him generously. after Dr. Kruger was gone. "Why don't you go swimming or something? I'll be O.K."

Mark was inclined to be generous, too, mellowed by the promise of tomorrow, and he claimed to have no interest in leaving the house today. A repetition of her suggestion, however, persuaded him. Five minutes later he was on the telephone, arranging with his friend, Tom Schultz, to meet at the pool at ten o'clock sharp.

Cathy stretched her arms above her head, wiggling her toes and flexing her fingers for exercise She slid herself over to a cooler part of the sheets and settled down to wait for tomorrow. From the basement came the steady chunk-chunk of the washing machine, making her think of stories of ocean liners in which the passengers always were aware of the constant throbbing of engines. She listened to Mark shout his plans to their mother, by way of the clothes chute in the bathroom, then to the bang of drawers and cupboards as he hunted for his mislaid swimming trunks.

Outdoors, a robin was chirping for rain. Cathy hoped that he would not get it—or else that he would get it now and not tomorrow. Maybe her father would take a day of vacation when her bandages came off, and they could celebrate her recovery by having a picnic at the amusement park. They didn't go there often, because Mark had a habit of becoming disgustingly ill on the second ride, even if it were only the merry-go-round. But, these days, everyone was eager to do everything that would please her.

The doorbell chimed. Mark whooped in answer and galloped to the front door. He was back in her room in a minute.

"Hey, Cathy, somebody to see you."

"How do you do, Cathy?" said a woman's voice, brisk and thin and totally unfamiliar.

Cathy wished Mark would learn to give her names instead of just saying "somebody." It was embarrassing to have to play guess-who from voices, especially if she didn't recognize them immediately and they belonged to people who thought she should. Yesterday she had called Mrs. Davis from across the street Mrs. Schultz by mistake, and Mrs. Davis had said, "Why, Cathy! You'll lose all your friends if you can't keep them sorted better than that!" in a tone that implied she was not altogether joking.

Cathy turned her face to this new puzzle and smiled to cover the doubt in her mind. "How do you do?"

"Isn't this pretty late in the morning for a big girl like you to be still lolling in bed?" the woman asked, without offering the slightest hint to her identity.

Cathy was stung. She supposed this was the visitor's manner of being humorous, but she didn't think it was funny at all! Heat prickled up her neck and cheeks

34

from inside. Certainly it was no fault of hers she was confined helpless in bed, and she resented the insinuation of wilful laziness in the word *lolling*.

"She can't get up until tomorrow," Mark said, a trifle belligerently. "She's been to the hospital and had an operation."

The woman advanced to the side of the bed. Her shoes squeaked, and her step was hard as a man's. "You must be making your mother a lot of extra work here," she said on a note Cathy imagined was meant to be bright, but which was accusing, nevertheless. "You ought to get on your feet as quickly as possible and start being of some help. A girl your age should be doing a great deal around the house."

"Yes," Cathy said meekly, her face burning hotter, "I will." She didn't know why she felt so apologetic or what business of this bossy stranger's her life was. The one thing she did know was that she needed reinforcements. "Mark, please tell Mom we have company."

Mark's feet pounded for the bathroom and the clothes chute. His shouts of, "Mom! Mom! Hurry upstairs!" were as urgent as a fire alarm. They also saved Cathy from being lectured further because they drowned out whatever else the woman might have had to say.

Cathy breathed easier at the sound of her mother's shushing Mark on her arrival in the kitchen. It was a satisfaction, also, to hear her confirm the fact that the nameless woman was a stranger by introducing herself as she reached the bedroom. "How do you do? I'm Mrs. Wheeler."

"I'm Miss Creel," the stranger said, and did not bother to acknowledge the *how-do-you-do*. "I am the field representative of the State School for the Blind at Burton. I thought I'd stop by to see Cathy today and talk to you about preparing her for admittance at the school."

Cathy's lungs snagged on an in-drawn gasp and would not come unstuck.

There was hardly less shock in her mother's voice. "Burton! Why, we hadn't considered— She has only been home from the hospital a week. I don't know who told you of us, but I'm afraid—"

"Your doctor filed a report. He is required to by law," Miss Creel said crisply. "I appreciate that you and your husband probably haven't looked much ahead concerning Cathy yet. We find that parents are often reluctant to face the facts or to do anything positive toward readjusting a child as long as they can avoid the issue. It's quite natural, and that's what I am here for. That is my job: to advise you what must be done."

"I thank you for your interest, but I can assure you that neither Cathy's father nor I have the least intention of avoiding the issue or neglecting what is best for her." Mrs. Wheeler spoke with a crispness Cathy had never heard from her before. It put even Miss Creel's to shame. "Mark, if you are meeting Tom at ten, you had better get started."

"O.K.." Mark said, but he did not move. Somehow, he had edged himself in between Miss Creel and the bed. "Where's Burton?"

Miss Creel's tone sweetened. "It's a town about a hundred miles from here. Nearly all the blind children in the state go to school there. It's like a boarding school. We find many of them are happier there than they would be at home. They learn to swim and play music and work at a trade, so that, when they graduate, they've become self-sufficient citizens, instead of being coddled into babyishness at home. We find it's very good for both the children and their families to live apart."

Cathy hunched her shoulders below the pillow, wishing she could shrink from sight. What kind of parents did Miss Creel know who would cast off their children like that, and what kind of children were they who preferred life at a boarding school to home? And what did Miss Creel think the Wheelers cared about the State School for the Blind, anyway? Just because Cathy couldn't see for a while, didn't mean she was—was that word!

"As I said," her mother repeated, "Mr. Wheeler and I haven't considered exactly what we will do about school this year. I'll tell him that you were here, but there is no point in you and I discussing the matter until I've talked to him."

"Of course," Miss Creel said. "I quite understand. September is less than a month away, though, and you ought to begin planning Cathy's continued education. She can't drop out of school altogether, you know, and the less school time she loses, the better. I'll leave you my phone number, in case you want to call me before I drop by again."

Her shoes creaked purposefully in the direction of the living room, leaving Cathy without the pretense of a good-by. The rustle of Mrs. Wheeler's starchy house dress followed, and Mark's sneakers padded quietly behind.

Cathy heard the murmur of talk in the living room, but she could make out nothing distinct. Presently, the front screen twanged shut, and there was the sharp little snap of the lock being thrust home. The dial of the telephone near the living room door began to whir rapidly, and her mother said, "Hello, Paul?" but the rest was lost under Mark's whistle as he passed the bedroom in search of his swimming gear and banged on out the back door to get his bike.

Cathy raised herself on one elbow, her ears straining not to miss the clunk of the telephone receiver when it was returned to its cradle. It seemed everyone had forgotten her, everyone but Miss Creel, who, she was sure, was determined to remember about her.

"Mom!" she called, her stomach cramped suddenly with a fear that plans perhaps were being made without consulting her. "I don't want to go to that school!"

The promptness of her mother's reply, spoken from the doorway, startled her. "I was just talking to your father, and he says not to worry yourself about it. It so happens that he phoned the school board office this morning. and the lady there told him there's no reason why you can't join your regular class at the high school here whenever you are ready. She thinks you should learn typing and Braille first, but there is a sight-saving class in one of the grade schools where they can teach you that. Daddy will give you the details when he gets home."

"What about Miss Creel? She said she'd be back."

"She can't force us to send you to Burton. It will be your own choice if you go. Daddy and I will stick by you whatever you decide, but the decision has to be yours, not ours."

Cathy grinned her relief. "I've decided." The statement grated on a small, hard core of resolution she hadn't known she possessed until Miss Creel's pointed digs had uncovered it. Her brows drew together in a frown that tugged at the strips of adhesive on her cheeks. "And I'm not going to be a coddled baby because I'm staying at home, either. Once I'm up and around again, I'll be the same as anybody else, and I won't ask favors of anyone. You watch!"

3

A WEEK LATER, Cathy sat on the back-yard swing, enjoying the flex of her shoulders and arms that drove her higher and higher while she took care her bare feet did not scrape on the swift-moving ground below. The August sun bored heat into her back and the top of her head, but it was a good feeling, and the rush of air the swing created kept her from getting too hot. Also, half the arc the swing made carried her into the heavy shade of the crab apple tree. Its coolness swept over her and receded like a wave.

Through the kitchen windows came the sounds of her mother preparing supper—the whish of water running from the tap, the clink of a lid on a pan, the sizzle of frying meat. The meat was chicken, her nose told her, and her tongue rolled itself together, anticipating.

Her nose was telling her a lot of things these days. For instance, it told her when there were pickles on the table, and if they were sweet or sour. It told her where to find her father's leather brief case in the front hall. It told her which plastic bottle on the bathroom shelf contained detergent, which shampoo and which her mother's facial cleanser. Now it was informing her that there were still roses in blossom near the garage, and that the earth around them was damp yet from Mark's latest capering with the hose. She supposed her nose must have been sniffing these odors for her all her life, otherwise she wouldn't recognize them so surely and easily, but until these past few days, she'd never paid much attention to its messages. It was queer.

A car door slammed shut in front of the house, and she began to let the swing die down, guessing her father was home and the call to supper would come soon. When she had slowed to where it was safe to drag her feet, though, and there was no voice from the kitchen, she started pumping again to have one final flight.

"Hey, Cathy!" Mark burst from the house, the rubber soles of his sneakers squeaking on the walk as he ran toward her. "Daddy's brought a whole bunch of stuff for you! Hurry up and see!"

"For me?" Cathy gave another thrust with her shoulders, rode the swing forward and jumped off onto the grass. "What kind of stuff?"

"Catherine Elizabeth Wheeler!" her mother cried from the kitchen window. "Whatever possessed you to do that? Do you want to break your neck?"

Cathy halted, almost as astonished as her mother. She had forgotten for a moment that she couldn't see. Jumping from the swing was a thing she had done so often that she could judge the right second by the feel of the breeze against her face and the lift of the seat. It was as automatic as tying her shoes without looking, or buttoning her blouse properly, or filling a drinking glass at the sink, or any of the other ordinary things she was finding she did not need sight for accomplishing unless she stopped to think how to do them. Since Dr. Kruger took off the bandages for her and freed her from the sensation of being hopelessly blindfolded, she had caught herself more than once forgetting that because her eyes were open and her mind producing a steady flow of pictures just behind them to match what she touched and smelled and heard didn't mean she was actually seeing.

But she didn't know how to explain it to anyone else. The truth was, she did not quite understand it herself, so she merely said, "I always jump when I'm in a hurry."

Her father laughed in the kitchen, sounding pleased. "Let her alone, Sue. I imagine she has a much better idea of what she can do than we have. Let her try her wings."

"At the rate she's going, she will need wings," her mother said. "I found her halfway up the willow this morning helping Mark pound nails in his tree house."

If her father commented on this, Cathy didn't hear, for she was seized by the hand and yanked impatiently toward the door.

"Come on," Mark said. "Don't you want to look at that stuff?"

He towed her in through the kitchen, around the corner of the dining room door and pressed her hand down on a square, leathery box in the middle of the living room floor. She wondered if it could be a suitcase of some sort. Her fingers quickly located a plastic handle on one side, and on another a pair of metal fastenings which Mark was already busily undoing.

"Raise the lid," he directed, using her hand to push

at it so as not to be accused of operating everything himself.

It was a thick lid, almost a box in itself, and it halted at right angles to the lower case. Her fingers brushed coarse matting, like the covering of a loud-speaker, then dropped to discover a turn table, tone arm and coil of electric cord.

"A record player?" she asked, and hoped there was no disappointment in her voice, but she had a record player bigger than this upstairs.

Her father sat himself on the floor beside her. "It's a talking book machine. I spent my lunch hour at the library today, and this is the result." He handed her a twelve-inch record disk. "Here's the first page of your book. Mark, plug the machine in, and we'll hear what happens."

He guided her hand to the two switches, one of which turned on the motor and controlled the volume. The other was for the turn table and to regulate the tone. She fitted the record onto the table, set the needle on carefully and, in a moment, a man's voice, distinct and pleasant, began speaking from the lid:

"Around the World in Eighty Days. By Jules Verne. Translated by George M. Towle. Introduction by Anthony Boucher. Recorded for the Library of Congress in the talking book studios of American Foundation for the Blind, Incorporated, with the kind permission of the publisher, Dodd, Mead and Company, Incorporated, solely for the use of the blind. Read by Alexander Scourby."

Cathy winced inwardly at the insensitive way in which people tossed around that ugly word *blind.* It jarred her nerves like chewing on sand each time she heard it, and she wished it might be struck from the language or forbidden by law.

But the voice was going on, reading the introduction now, in vigorous, cultivated tones that captured her interest because the man sounded so interested himself. She loved being read aloud to, anyway, almost as much as she loved reading to herself, and she had been on the waiting list at the neighborhood library for *Around the World in Eighty Days* ever since school was out.

"There're only seven more records in this box," Mark announced, shoving a carton of heavy cardboard against Cathy's knee. "They must play a long time on each side if he can read a whole book on just eight records."

"They play about twenty minutes per side, the librarian told me," Mr. Wheeler said. "And when Cathy's done with this book, she packs it up in the box, we drop if off at the post office, and the librarian sends her another one by parcel post delivery, free of charge. Both the books and the machine belong to the Library of Congress and are loaned out free to anyone who needs them." He chuckled. "That includes people whose parents are headed for laryngitis from too much reading aloud. Here is the glory of modern machines, Cathy: this thing won't quit at the most exciting part because its voice is tired, not while you have records to feed it."

"More power to it!" Cathy's mother laughed and stooped to flip through the records in the box. "I hope they aren't too strict about that 'solely for the use of' clause, because I may be tempted to do some listening myself if it's on when I'm ironing or scrubbing floors. But what odd records! Did you notice, Cathy? They have regular print labels on one side, but only bumps or dots on the other. Do you suppose that is Braille?"

Cathy switched off the machine and picked up the record to examine it. There were indeed dots on it, like bubbles in the plastic, but no sweep of her fingers could detect the least hint of a pattern in them. If this were Braille, it must take a person years to learn it. She would be able to see again before she could ever make sense out of this.

Her father heaved himself to his feet. "That brings me to the other part of my surprise. The librarian gave me a special set of books, Cathy, so that, if you want to learn Braille, your mother and I can teach you without having to learn it first ourselves. You learn from this one, and we check you from the exact same lesson in an ink-print book."

Into Cathy's lap, he lowered the most enormous book she had encountered in her life. It rivaled the size of an unabridged dictionary. Its pages were broader than those of the *Saturday Evening Post,* but to her surprise, it weighed not much more than an ordinary book. She opened it at random to rub her fingers over the myriads of tiny, raised dots that sprinkled the page as thickly and haphazardly as poppy seeds on a roll. A tingle went through her that was half excitement, half dismay.

Ruefully, she said, "If I'd had ten extra cents last summer, I probably could have read this already. There was a book of codes in the drugstore—Morse code, wigwag signals, stuff like that—and it had Braille in it, too, but Pete and I only had fifty cents between us, and he wanted an ice cream cone first, before he bought anything else. Otherwise we'd have had it."

"In that case," her mother said, starting for the kitchen, "I guess you can put off the learning a little while longer, until you've had supper, anyway. Come on, everybody. It's all ready."

It was a mouth-watering supper, but Cathy would have settled for a sandwich and a glass of milk that could be gulped down quickly and wouldn't leave so many dishes to wash. In the back of her mind was a ripening suspicion that she might have been a trifle rash in insisting, two nights ago, that she was as capable as ever of helping with the dishes. She couldn't very well skip out on the job after only two days, not and stick to her determination to ask no favors, but she wondered if a little more thought might not have shown her ways less bothersome and quite as effective of proving she wasn't coddled.

At length the dishes were done, however, and she was at liberty to join her father on the davenport, and to examine the huge volume of dots while her father read her the introduction in the ink-print book. The Braille system, it said, was based on a block of six dots, three dots high and two dots wide, called a cell. Every letter and symbol in the system was made of some combination or other of these six dots. The top dot on the left was *a;* that one and the middle dot on the left were *b;* the two top dots were *c.* Also, there were three grades of standard Braille: grade one, which included only the alphabet, numbers and punctuation; grade one-and-a-half, which added symbols, called contractions, that stood for things like *the, and, for, en* and *ing;* and grade two, which added more complicated contractions, plus word abbreviations such as *alt* for *altogether* and *rcv* for *receive.*

With the assistance of Mark, who was breathing down her neck in his eagerness to be edified, too, Cathy found the examples in her book and pushed her finger to and fro over them until she feared she would squash the dots flat. They were such tiny dots that it was as much as she could do to distinguish between one and half a dozen, let alone feeling which sets contained only two or three and in what combinations, but a half hour of experimenting showed her that the ball of her forefinger rubbed lightly across the patterns, instead of being pressed numb into the paper, was likely to do the best job of seeing for her.

That was the start of what became routine evening lessons during the weeks that followed. Mark's enthusiasm for the Braille system was exhausted by the end of the second day, but Cathy could not resist the challenge of mastering anything that was so much like a secret code. For an hour each morning, sitting cross-legged in the shade of the crab apple tree or, if the weather was rainy, curled up in a corner of the davenport, she memorized the characters of the day's lesson, and each evening she read the lesson aloud while her mother or her father checked her by looking at the corresponding page in the ink-print book. Her memory was good, and she liked problems that called for concentration, but it was heavy going at times, especially when she advanced from single letters to reading words. Acknowledging a lone dot as *a* was one thing, and a pair of dots close together like a dash as *c*, and an arrangement of four that reminded her of a stylized cactus as *t*. It was entirely another matter to recognize a dash, a dot and a cactus as *cat*, even when she spelled it out, letter by letter, and tried fooling her mind into thinking she was viewing the letters in print. She did make progress, though, and it was fun knowing something no one else did. What had scared her that day in Dr. Kruger's office was the shock of what he meant, not the idea of learning Braille itself. And when she tired of chewing away on *cat* and *dog*—which was spelled with a corner, an arrowhead and a square block —there were always the talking books to do her real reading for her.

All the same, it took alertness and strict attention to weld communication links between her fingers, ears, nose and mind that were keen enough to transmit the messages that were the business of her eyes before, and she didn't appreciate Mrs. Davis's brushing off the effort by remarking of her to her mother one afternoon: "Isn't Nature marvelous? Lose your sight, and, immediately, Nature sharpens the rest of your senses to where they're practically superhuman to compensate for it. It's a miracle that just seems to happen overnight!"

Cathy squirmed on her chair, wondering if beans were ever insulted when people marveled at their ability to sprout right side up, even if you planted them wrong side down! She could invent no graceful method of escaping Mrs. Davis's flow of admiration, however, until Mark shouted in at the kitchen door, "Hey, Cathy? I put air in your tires. Want to try riding your bike?"

She was out of the house and on her way to the garage in a second, grateful to her mother for saying only, "Stay in the alley or on the quiet streets. And tell Mark to keep an eye peeled for cars."

As she hesitated at the top of the terrace, her feet hunting for the steps down to the alley, she heard Mrs. Davis's voice booming, "Susan Wheeler, I don't see how you dare! If I had a child like that, I'd put her in an institution where she would be with her own kind, and I'd know she was safe and in trained hands. I wouldn't have the responsibility of keeping her at home."

Cathy ran down the stairs and in through the side door of the garage, banging the door hard behind her. The old busybody! What was everybody in such a steam to get her locked up somewhere by herself for? A person would think she was feeble-minded or a homicidal maniac or something! Well, the decision was hers to make, and they wouldn't catch her deciding in favor of an institution.

Mark wheeled her bike to her. "You're headed O.K., now. I'll ride ahead and yell 'right' and 'left,' and you can follow and not smash into anything."

It sounded simple, but, in practice, it did not work out quite as they imagined. Mark's notion of what the directions *right* and *left* were agreed to indicate was rather hazy, and he was inclined to substitute, "No, stop! Turn!" in a moment of crisis. But his chain clanked against his chain guard on every revolution of the wheel, and, after a few false starts and screeching halts, Cathy found its noise was as reliable a guide as she needed.

This was the first time she had been on a bicycle since she went to the hospital, and she had almost forgotten how it was to stretch her legs rhythmically and steadily to the full without shuffling for secure footing or pausing spasmodically, for fear of knocking a shin or a temple on something lurking unseen ahead. The sensation of minute but effortless balance, of power mounting and yielding beneath her control, the familiar bump of tires rolling over the seams of the pavement, the smell of warm tar and the crackle of the heat bubbles in it were as thrilling as though she'd never experienced them before.

She and Mark cruised the length of the alley a dozen

times or so and were about to venture onto the street when Mark slammed on his brakes, calling back to her, "Hold it! Here comes Pete Sheridan, acting like he's on a speedway."

"Pete!" Cathy eased the pedals into reverse, not putting her foot to the ground until she had coasted up beside her brother. "Where?"

The approaching rattle of Pete's bike basket told her without Mark's having to answer, and a fresh excitement danced through her. She knew that Pete must have been home from his parent's summer cottage for several days, but the last she'd seen or heard of him was the day they said good-by after her birthday picnic. It was her fault as much as his, for she'd done nothing to keep track of him because of an odd sort of shyness that gripped her at the thought of having to explain the details of what had happened and what she had been doing since he left. Now that he was nearly upon her, though, she realized how much she had missed him, and how glad she would be to pick up their friendship on the old terms again. Mark had been filling the gap pretty well, had actually been more of a pal than a brother lately, but Mark was only eight, after all—and he wasn't Pete.

"Hi, Pete!" she hailed him as the bike rattled abreast of them.

"Hi, Pete," Mark echoed on a flatter note.

The bike skidded to the customary tire-squealing, Pete Sheridan stop. "Hi, Mark." He cleared his throat, as though he were slightly embarrassed. "Hi, Cathy. How are you?"

"Fine," she answered happily. "How are you? How was the cottage?"

"O.K., I guess."

Cathy judged he must have been reading one of his books on Indians again, or maybe the one about the Spartan soldiers of ancient Greece, by the care he was taking to use as few words as possible. Probably he was wearing his Northwest Mounty's whistle on its braided thong around his neck, too. She grinned at him, ignoring a tiny needle of irritation that wanted to protest his stiffness. "Where've you been since you got home? I haven't seen you for ages."

"Yeah, well—" Pete scuffed his shoe on the pavement, and a pebble went rolling. "I haven't been around much. I've been kind of busy. Doing stuff. I'll be seeing you."

"Come on over when you get the chance," Cathy said warmly. "I have a whole lot of things to show you. You like *The Grand Canyon Suite,* don't you? And I have a new record player that's only for talking, and some books—"

"Never mind," Mark cut in. "He's gone."

Cathy choked off her voice and stood listening, her mouth still open, her hands growing sticky moist on the cold steel of her handle bars. The rattle of Pete's basket was retreating down the alley as if propelled by a jet engine.

"I didn't hear him go," she said—and hated herself for the simpleton she must have looked, chattering to empty air.

"Pete Sheridan is a skunk cabbage," Mark said, stating an opinion which had the conviction of long standing with him. "He's been around plenty since he got home from their cottage, but he won't ever say hello any more. He just walks by and stares like he was at the zoo, or else ducks his head and pretends he doesn't hear if he thinks anybody's noticing him." He

51

kicked at a pebble and sent it skipping into the grass at the pavement's edge. "Which way shall we ride from here? Up toward Ridge Street or toward the boulevard?"

Cathy swallowed . . . and had to swallow again before her throat would loosen up on her answer. "I'm tired of riding, I guess. Let's go home."

She wheeled her bike in a tight circle and raised herself onto the seat as Mark, without argument, clanked past her to swing into the lead. The attention she had to focus on steering by sound gradually drew the fire out of her mortification, but it left a sore spot of disappointment that common sense warned her not to prod too far. Pete was a funny person, moody and hard to predict. Maybe he would be over in a day or so, anyhow, once he'd had a chance to think about it. But one thing was sure: if he came, it would be his own doing. She would never, never again ask him to visit her.

Mark rode off as she parked her bike in the garage, and she climbed the terrace steps slowly, in no rush to be anywhere in particular. A voice, thin and piercing as a mosquito whine, stabbed into her ears from the house.

"I quite understand how difficult this situation is for you and your husband, Mrs. Wheeler. Perhaps I understand it more than you do yourselves because I can be objective about it, instead of obscuring my vision with sentiment and emotion. That is why I hate to see you bent on making a mistake like this. The place for a handicapped child is among other handicapped children, where it can be trained by those specially trained themselves for the job. I am afraid you will have to recognize eventually that pretending Cathy can continue living your concept of a normal life can only do more harm than good."

Cathy dropped to her hands and knees on the steps and sidled crabwise to the wall of the garage, where she knew she was hidden from the kitchen windows by the honeysuckle bush at the top of the terrace. It was a month since she had first heard that voice, but it was cut into her memory. Miss Creel had returned.

Another minute of breathless listening told her Miss Creel was somewhere in the front of the house, probably the living room, and could not spot her anyway. Her mother's voice was a faint murmur, replying.

"Well," Miss Creel said, as if she were weary of arguing, "I do hope for your sakes that your plans work out as you expect, but I can't say that I honestly believe they can. I'll be in town again at Thanksgiving time, and I'll stop by then."

Cathy wished she dared shout, "Wait till you're asked!" but she stayed hunched down behind the bush like a rabbit until an automobile door slammed, and the car roared off up the street. The decision was hers to make, though, and no one else's, and she hugged the knowledge of it to her like a magic charm. And school opened day after tomorrow!

Nevertheless, Cathy did not feel absolutely safe until the opening day of the new school did arrive—and passed by without a hitch. She was nervous getting on the school bus that pulled up in front of the house for her that morning, but the ride, which circled the city to collect various blind, crippled, or deaf children for special classes in different schools, was too long and the bus driver, who creaked in a leather jacket that smelled like horses, cracked too many jokes for her to keep on being very worried. At the door of the school, she was met by Mrs. Knudtson, who introduced herself as the sight-saving teacher and guided Cathy up a flight of wooden stairs to an empty classroom on the second floor.

"There are five other pupils who will be in this room, too," Mrs. Knudtson explained, in a soft, rich voice that had a smile deep inside it. "Two are little first-grade girls, one is a fifth-grade boy, and Donna and Jerry are both in seventh grade. But they all have classes with their own grades in other rooms most of the time, and only come in here for lessons in Braille or typing, or to study. They tell me you belong in ninth grade, Cathy, so, as this school doesn't go beyond the eighth, I'm afraid you'll have to resign yourself to me for company and this room for scenery. Now then, let's get busy doing something before the others start popping in and making mischief."

They got started on Braille, and Cathy glowed at Mrs. Knudtson's praises of her reading ability, laborious and stumbling though it was. Later, Mrs. Knudtson set her at a typewriter, showed her how to place her hands correctly on the smooth keys and set her to typing *dfcv, dfcv,* over and over, until she knew their positions by heart and had five lines done perfectly. In the afternoon, the teacher gave Cathy a sheet of heavy paper and a pair of tools for writing Braille, a Braille slate and a stylus. The slate proved to be two pieces of aluminum, joined by a hinge. Four lines of twenty-seven complete Braille cells were stamped into the back piece, and the same number were cut out of the top piece, so that only their outlines were left. When the paper was fitted between these two pieces, the stylus, which was like a wooden knob from a drawer with a nail stuck out of one end, punched the proper dots into the paper by following the edges of the cutouts, while the stamped hollows beneath kept them from being pushed clear through and becoming holes.

Cathy was fascinated by this process of writing. Because the dots were punched from the back of the paper and appeared on the bottom side, the characters had to be formed backwards, and written from right to left. It was as tricky as mirror writing, but simpler because there were just six dots per cell to choose from, although, of course, a slip of the stylus poked in a dot that didn't belong and changed the whole letter. She punched away busily, experimenting and practicing, delighted to find that, in spite of her slowness at reading, she could write like this nearly as fast as a person could use a pencil.

Then, suddenly, the first day was over. The second went by even more swiftly. So did the third and the fourth. By the second week, the school hours had worn themselves into a routine that seemed as old as forever and definite as a highway.

In the midst of all this activity, Cathy forgot about Pete. At least, she shoved him to the back of her mind and let him be walled in by more important things—like going to school and going to church, washing dishes, wrestling with Mark and planning sometimes how she would manage next semester, when she would have enough Braille and typing skill to join her class at the high school.

She wasn't much surprised, though, one crisp Saturday morning at the end of September, to hear his, "Hi, Cathy," behind her as she was about to carry into the house a box of talking book records the parcel postman had just brought. If nothing else, curiosity would weaken Pete, and the mail truck was a weekly visitor at the Wheelers' these days.

"Hi, Pete," she responded casually, pretending it was of no interest to her whether he was here or not. "I have to take these in and see what they are. Want to come, too?"

He came, and, for a while, it was the same as it had always been between them. Pete examined the talking book machine and listened to part of a record—Jack London's *Call of the Wild* this time—and they talked and laughed and traded ideas. But only for a while. There was a fine thread of strain running through everything they did and said, as though they were half-way strangers, watching and being cautious of each other, Cathy thought. This grew into open restlessness as soon as Pete tired of the records and had looked at the Braille books.

"Man!" he exclaimed abruptly. "It's almost lunch time! I better get home and finish mowing the lawn or my dad will skin me."

He lunged for the front door, and Cathy scrambled after him, bumping her elbow sharply on the corner of the television set in her haste to keep up. "What are you doing this afternoon?" she asked at the door, hating to have him leave regardless of their awkwardness.

"Oh, I don't know. Errands probably." He slid out the door and jumped the two steps to the walk. "See you around."

Cathy leaned her forehead against the screen for a moment, listening to the soft thud of his feet running across the grass toward his house, before she closed the inner door. There was a cool edge in the wind, a tang of wood smoke and dry grass and dead leaves, although there weren't many leaves on the ground yet. Next week would be October. Next Saturday would be— Pete's birthday! Why hadn't she realized that earlier?

56

She could have asked him about his party, or mentioned it, anyhow. Asking would have been silly, because she'd shared such a lot of his birthday parties that she knew their formula as well as he did. Now that he'd broken the ice separating them, though, maybe they could get together during the week to discuss details.

But Monday night the school bus was late in bringing her home. Tuesday and Wednesday were sodden with cold rain. Thursday evening the family went to Grandma Wheeler's for supper.

"Hey, guess what," Mark said Friday night, pouring a drink of water into himself at the kitchen sink while she was laying silverware on the table for supper. "I just saw Pete and Mr. Sheridan loading their car with camping stuff. They're taking off first thing tomorrow for a weekend at Chippewa State Park. That's the swellest birthday present I ever heard of!"

Then Pete must not be having a party this year. Cathy placed a knife carefully, cutting side in, to the right of her father's plate, disappointment pinching her. Yet, in a way, she was relieved, too. She'd been almost afraid that— Well, there was no sense putting a name to it since it wasn't true.

After supper and the dishes, she tucked herself into her bedroom chair to listen to the end of *Call of the Wild*. Once or twice she thought she heard scraps of laughter and talking somewhere outside, but the story was too absorbing for her to give more than fleeting notice to other sounds until the record was done. Everything was quiet as she switched off the turn table, but before she could change the record, a burst of squeals and yelling broke forth that was loud even through the panes of the closed windows. It had the ring of a party.

She turned off the machine, and ran downstairs,

grabbing up her sweater from the back of a kitchen chair on her way by. The heavy breath of charcoal smoke met her the instant she stepped into the yard. It was twined like ribbons in and around the breeze blowing from the direction of Sheridans' yard, and with it were mixed the shouts and chuckles of young voices, voices strange to her and voices she recognized as Pete's and those of Pete's school buddies—Jim and Rich and Joan Norton, the girl Pete always asserted he couldn't stomach. There were other girls, too, a thing unheard of at Pete's house because, Cathy excepted, he disdained them all, but there they were, shrill and giggly and, judging by the racket, having glorious fun.

Loneliness bit into Cathy so hard that the pain of it nearly broke her in two. She didn't question why Pete should have forgotten to invite her to a party that included everyone else. Her only thought was that she just had to be part of the fun, no matter what it cost to get there.

It must still be light outside, at any rate, light enough to see a person in her yard from the Sheridan place, only three doors away. Maybe if she made herself too obvious to ignore, Pete would call her over. She walked to the swing and stepped onto the seat, deciding to pump standing up, in order to be as visible as possible. In case she was mistaken about the visibility, she began to sing gaily in time to the bending of her arms and knees:

"Sailing, sailing, over the bounding main . . ."

In a pause to catch her breath, Pete's yell came enthusiastically across the yards. "Hey, you kids! The alley's the diamond from our garage to the one next door. Girls against the boys!"

She let the swing die down to a standstill. By the

time she stepped to the ground, bats were clunking on the alley pavement. Boys were shouting directions, marking positions.

Joan Norton cried out plaintively, "That's not fair! Ladies first."

Cathy scuffed her feet through the grass until her shoes scraped on the cement walk. Maybe if she went out in the alley, just kind of strolling along . . .

Someone was running up the Sheridans' terrace steps. "Be back in a sec," Pete yelled. "That extra mitt's right inside, under my bed."

"Hi, Pete!" she called, trying to sound casual, but putting the whole strength of her lungs into the hail.

For an answer, there was a cheer from the alley. Somebody had hit a home run.

Cathy dug her nails into her palms, clenching her fists in the pockets of her sweater to concentrate power for a louder blast, but pride caught at her voice and froze it to silence. The Sheridans' back door banged shut. Reopened. Feet galloped down to the alley. A cry of "Strike three!" arose, and a cheer, while she stood like a worthless old tree stump, motionless and hollow.

"Pete!" Mr. Sheridan trumpeted from where Cathy knew the outdoor fireplace to be. "Better cancel the game until later. These hot dogs are looking for anyone that's hungry."

Cathy turned, fumbled along the rear of the house to locate the doorknob, and crept in through the kitchen. Her mother spoke to her from the living room, but she made believe not to hear and went on quietly upstairs to her room. This wasn't a time when sympathy could help, or companionship, or anything.

She wilted onto her knees in front of her chair and

pillowed her head on her arms in the seat. Her lashes grew wet, then her cheeks, and then the sleeve of her sweater, but they weren't the swift, hot tears she'd wept in fright on her birthday and in the hospital. These were big, slow tears of hurt. They hardly buckled her shoulders in their swelling, but each was rooted deep in an ache that tore wider at every breath.

Nobody bothered her for perhaps an hour, but she was still sitting on the floor, although her eyes were dry by now, when she heard Mark tiptoeing warily up the stairs.

"Hey, Cathy?" he said from the hall, in a half whisper, as though he thought she might be asleep. "Daddy says if you'll get ready, he'll take us to the Milk Jug for a malt or a sundae. You want to go?"

She didn't. There was nothing she wanted less, in fact. But a trip to the Milk Jug was a splendid event in Mark's eyes, and if she wouldn't go, probably no one would. It was wrong not to consider how other people would feel before you slashed them aside for your own selfish comfort.

She grubbed a handkerchief out of her pocket and blew her nose into it. "O.K. In a minute."

"Gee, thanks!" Mark whirled for the stairs. On the landing, he stopped a split second to declare in tones that sizzled indignation, "That Pete Sheridan is a dirty rat."

Cathy echoed him inwardly, but that didn't change matters any. Because she could not see, she was different, too different for Pete to like having her around. And if Pete, whom she had considered her very best friend, felt that way about her, how would it be with the kids in her classes at high school? She didn't have the nerve to face it.

Pushing herself to her feet, she went to the dresser and began pulling a comb through her hair. Already she knew what the solution must be. When Miss Creel returned at Thanksgiving, she would tell her she had decided to go to the blind school at Burton.

4

"I THINK YOU'VE made a wise decision, Cathy," Miss Creel said as her car slowed to round a curve. "Burton isn't like living at home, of course, but entering now, at the end of Christmas vacation, instead of at the beginning of the new semester, will give you an excellent chance to become adjusted to everything before your real classes start. I know you won't regret it."

Cathy squirmed herself a little straighter on the front seat, wondering if she dared ask how much farther they had to go before they reached the school. It seemed like days since she kissed her mother good-by and was shut into this car for the long drive to Burton. She was having twinges of lonesomeness in spite of Miss Creel's unrelenting flow of conversation. Or maybe because of it. Miss Creel had been doing her utmost to be affable the whole length of the drive, but she did it as if it were a duty, not something that came from genuine good will. Cathy could not quite work up a glow toward her, although she did want Miss Creel—or somebody—to be her friend, now that home was so far away.

Things would be better when they arrived at the school, Cathy told herself. There would be more for her to do and think about than just perching on a plastic-covered car seat that insisted on sliding her down on the small of her back, no matter how rigidly she sat. Actually, once she decided on Burton, she had almost looked forward to this day. Her head was full of stories she'd read about boarding schools, all of them tales of adventures, special friendships and gay times. It well might be that fun and excitement were in store for her, if ever this ride should come to an end.

Miss Creel slowed again. Her turn signals clicked on, and Cathy slid up against the door as the car made a sharp right.

"We've just entered the city of Burton," Miss Creel said cheerfully. "This is the main street we are on. Probably you'll be walking down here yourself one of these days, to go shopping."

She patted the horn suddenly, stepped briefly on the brake, then rolled into normal speed once more, chuckling to herself. "That was one of our girls. Francie Adams. She's a sweet little thing. She always waves. I imagine you'll be put in her dormitory, because you'll both be in my ninth-grade English class."

This last bit of information startled Cathy. She had not been warned that Miss Creel not only rounded up students for the state school but taught them as well. For a sinking moment, she wondered if Miss Creel perhaps *was* the school—but there was another point that required explaining first.

"How did that girl—Francie Adams—how did she know it was your horn? How did she know whom to wave at?"

"Francie has very good vision," Miss Creel said, as

though this need not surprise anyone. "That is, good for our school. She reads large print quite easily, and even some smaller print. Most of our pupils have some vision, although not enough for them to get along in a public school, but Francie is an exceptionally bright girl. You will like her."

It sounded as though brightness depended on a person's amount of vision in Miss Creel's opinion, but Cathy pushed the thought away. She had every intention of liking Francie Adams the minute she had the chance, and, if possible, she wanted to like Miss Creel, too. Probably the first step in that direction would be to stop believing Miss Creel meant everything she said exactly as she happened to say it. Or maybe the first step was to get over being afraid of her, or anyhow so nervous in her presence that it was genuine hard labor not to twist your hands or kick your feet or fidget all the time.

Groping for something fitting to hold up her share of the conversation, Cathy said, "I hope Francie will like me."

"That will depend a great deal on you and how quickly you adapt to life here. If you take pains to learn, as I'm sure you will, I don't see that you need have any doubts about Francie or the other nice girls," Miss Creel said, laying a faint but definite stress on the word *nice*.

Cathy wondered if there were some girls at Burton who weren't nice, but there was a touch of the old crispness in Miss Creel's voice that did not invite further questioning.

The car had been zigzagging around a few more corners, and now was following a very curving road. . . . Snow crunched under the wheels, then, with a mild jerk and a click of the key in the ignition, Miss Creel brought the car to a halt.

"Here we are," she announced. "Right at the front steps. They are straight ahead of you when you get out. Wait a minute, and I'll have your suitcase for you."

Cathy lost no time in opening the door and climbing out. She had a weird feeling that she had been locked away inside a space capsule for a month and was setting the first human foot on the surface of the moon. Brittle, frozen snow crackled under her boots, digging hard peaks of ice upward into the soles, but the shiver that tingled through her blood was not altogether a result of the sharp January wind that greeted her.

The car trunk banged shut, and Miss Creel joined her. "Here is your suitcase, Cathy. Bring it along. The steps are directly in front of you."

Obediently, Cathy grasped the handle of the big suitcase and shoved a foot forward until the toe bumped against a step. She wished Miss Creel would lend an arm as a guide, but her companion's boots were already clump-clumping up the steps, and there was nothing to do but shuffle on after her, as rapidly as was prudent on the unfamiliar path.

"Here is the door," Miss Creel said and, giving a determined grunt, produced a drawn-out squeal of hinges that told Cathy this was a door of a size to be reckoned with. "I'll hold it for you. Hurry, before you let all the heat out!"

Cathy hurried, stumbling over an uneven mat just inside and grazing her left knee on the corner of a chair or bench or some other such piece of low furniture. She staggered on to recapture her balance, then shuffled ahead a few paces more until, for sheer want of direction, she came to a halt, guessing she was about in the middle of what seemed to be a large room or reception hall, and sure that she must be sticking out in all her awkwardness like a broken thumb.

Warmth surrounded her, making her chilled face burn, but the air was sluggish and heavy, and what impressed her most was the peculiar odor that was as much a part of it as the heat. It was a complex odor—a blend of ancient varnish, of sour scrubbing compound, of steam-hot iron radiators, of old meals long since eaten and of smells too vague to put a name to—a dingy odor that painted for her mind's eye a room of frowning dark woodwork and discolored walls. Even through her boots she could tell that the linoleum on the floor was worn rough in spots, and that the floor boards underneath were warped into ridges and hollows.

To the right of her was a group of three or four girls, who chorused, "Hello, Miss Creel. Welcome back!" as though they'd been rehearsing it. That their gathering place was a switchboard was revealed by a buzz, a click and one of the girls interrupting her giggle to say smoothly, "Good morning, State School for the Blind."

"Hello, girls," Miss Creel said in a tone that was pure business. "I'm glad you're here, Georgie. This is a new girl, Cathy Wheeler, and she'll be rooming with you. Take her upstairs and get her settled, won't you? I'm sure the house mother has put another bed in for her, hasn't she?"

"Yep, but she had to squeeze plenty to get it there," Georgie said in a hoarse voice that, for some reason, reminded Cathy of a frog. "Come on, Cathy. This way."

"Go on, Cathy," Miss Creel prompted. Not a trace remained of her earlier cordiality. It was as if she left her pleasantness in her car, to be used only when she

66

was closed in too small a space for her ordinary personality to be comfortable, or maybe safe. "And lift your feet off the floor when you walk. Don't shuffle. That's one of the first things we teach here."

Cathy swallowed, aware that she was the focus of the watchful silence that had descended on the switchboard. What a blessing if one of those valleys in the uneven floor would just sink low enough to hide her! Her clumsy winter boots weighed like cement blocks, but she lifted them high above the slightest chance of scuffing as, carrying her suitcase at an angle in front of her for a bumper to protect her from whatever shin or head traps might be jutting out ahead, she trailed after Georgie's quick, slapping steps, across the unknown expanses of the reception hall and a narrower passage beyond.

"The stairs start here," Georgie said. In spite of its hoarseness, her voice was cheerful and not unfriendly. "We live on the fourth floor. That's six flights up."

Loaded down with boots, winter coat and the suitcase, Cathy was out of breath by the top of the sixth flight. She was resolved to co-operate in everything and to find nothing wrong anywhere, if she could manage it, but she couldn't help the *"Whew!"* that escaped her when she dropped the suitcase in the room to which Georige led her.

"Some climb, isn't it?" Georgie said appreciatively. "Wait until you remember something vital's been left up here five minutes before you have a class on the first floor. That's your bed there, next to the door."

Cathy extended a cautious hand, trying not to look as if she were groping, and immediately located the smooth iron tubing of the foot of a narrow cot. "Thanks," she said, easing around the end of it to seat herself on the edge. It had about as little give to it as a piano bench, but she put her whole strength into sounding lively and undismayed as she bent to unzip and pull off her boots. "There, that's better. I feel ten pounds lighter."

"You can put them in the closet. It's to the left of the head of your bed," Georgie said. "You can put your coat in there and other stuff that needs hanging, too, only there's not an awful lot of room. There's a bureau on the other side of the door for the rest of your things, but you'll have to share it with Francie Adams. Probably you'd better take the bottom two drawers, because she always fills up the top three."

Shedding her coat and scarf on the bed, Cathy rose and nudged her suitcase forward until it snagged itself on what proved to be the bureau in question. "I might as well get moved in right now," she said, kneeling on the floor to open the upper of the two bottom drawers. "It won't take long, because I'm going home this week-end, so I didn't bring much." More to keep the conversation going than anything else, she added, "Are there three of us to this room, then? You and Francie Adams and me?"

"Three!" Georgie echoed, the rasp in her voice derisive. She struck a metallic clank from the foot of the bedstead she was evidently perched on. "That'll be the day! There's seven in here now, counting you. The smallest room on this floor has five in it, and they'll pack in more if old Creepy Creel can scrounge up some extras. They say she and the school get a boost in state money for every new pupil, and I don't doubt it. She's out in the state half the time, hunting down innocent victims."

Cathy paused in the act of tucking her comb and hair brush in a handy corner of the drawer, a sudden

68

tightness in her chest, but before she could decide whether Georgie was joking or in earnest about the victim part, the rough voice went blithely on: "Anyway, there's seven of us here in 410. There's you and me— I'm Georgie Willis, by the way—and Francie Adams and Emma Johnson and Hope Cowley and Ida Smith, and Daisy Brewer. Don't leave any money or jewelry or stuff like that around where Daisy can find it, because she has a habit of taking things. A couple years ago she just missed being expelled for taking ten dollars of Francie's, but, even though everybody knew it was Daisy and the police were called in and everything, nobody could prove it, and that night the money turned up in Francie's purse again, where it hadn't been half an hour earlier." Georgie waited a minute for the effect of this to sink in, then yawned. "It's nearly time for dinner, so when you're through there, I might as well show you where the washroom is while we're up here."

The washroom was the first door at the bend in the hall. Cathy was heartened by the ample flow of hot water at the sink she used, although she had to dry her hands by flapping them in the air because Georgie had forgotten to mention that each girl's towel and wash cloth were hung on a rack over the back of her bedside chair.

"If you kick your foot to the side, you'll hit the bathtub," Georgie said. "You're supposed to take a shower or a bath here every day but they don't check too closely on the fourth floor. On the third floor, the house mother stands right there to inspect the kids every morning, but those are the ones in the lower grades. . . . Come on! That's the bell for dinner, and I'm starved."

Cathy raced down the stairs with Georgie, holding

lightly to the rail and laughing to show she was a good sport. But it was not so easy to fool herself. There was a fast-growing leak in her enthusiasm for boarding schools, and the dining-room situation in which she soon found herself did nothing to plug it.

"You might as well sit here at the first table until somebody assigns you a place," Georgie said, nudging her against a steel folding chair. "I'm two tables down."

"It sounds empty in here," Cathy said.

"It practically is. Since school isn't officially in session until eight tomorrow morning, most of the kids won't get in until this evening, if they can help it. It doesn't matter, though, because there's no talking during meals, anyway. A rule. If you want anything, just wave your hand in the air and an attendant will come. Don't try leaving without me, because, if you happen to wander over into the boys' half of the dining room, you'll catch trouble."

In lonely silence, Cathy accepted the plate that was set before her. Miss Creel had warned her on the ride to Burton that, "The school food is all very wholesome and nourishing, but it is institution food. It has to be cooked in large quantities, which means you must not expect it to taste like what you are used to at home."

The proof of this met Cathy's fork in the form of two round, hard knobs of potatoes, slippery in coats of cooling grease, and in a dry slab of meat, its flavor too nondescript for her to be sure what kind of animal it came from. She had been nearly as hungry as Georgie at the start, but a few bites took the edge off her appetite in a hurry. Luckily, dessert was a dish of ice cream, and she was able to fill up fairly well on that, but by then her insides were beginning to squeeze themselves smaller, anyway.

"How long have you been here?" she asked Georgie as they walked out of the dining room together.

"About five years, I guess," Georgie said. "Since I was ten."

Cathy wanted to ask her if she liked it, but Georgie might take this as a criticism. Cathy wasn't sure herself she didn't mean it that way, for it was fairly plain that Georgie was perfectly contented and at home here.

"Hey, don't start down there!" Georgie said quickly, and grabbed Cathy's arm to stop her from turning where she thought the stairs ought to be. "You'll get yourself in a pile of trouble."

Cathy sprang back, her mind flashing a picture of a gaping manhole or yawning trap door opening in the floor to swallow her at the next step. "Why? What's wrong?"

Georgie giggled, lowering her voice and pulling Cathy to the stairway. "Don't sound so scared. It's just an imaginary line you're not supposed to cross or you'll be campused. It wouldn't matter so much except that old Creepy Creel is standing there in the hall with her hawk eyes peeled. Come on up to the room, and I'll explain it."

Cathy's curiosity wouldn't let her wait that long. "What do you mean by an imaginary line?" she asked when the second flight of stairs assured her of a whole floor between them and Miss Creel. "What's it for? And how do you know where it is?"

"You better learn where it is," Georgie said, puffing from the climb in a fashion that suggested her odd voice was not the only heavy thing about her. "Any time you get caught stepping over it, especially by the house mother or Creepy Creel, you can be in for trouble. It cuts across the hall from the girls' door of the dining

71

room to the door of the library. There's another one from the boys' door of the dining room, but you don't have to worry about that. Don't ever go down that hall unless you're on the way to class."

"But why not?" Cathy persisted as they began the next flight of stairs. "What's down there?"

Georgie let her breath out in a slow hiss. "Boys!"

Cathy waited the length of another flight, but when Georgie offered no further explanation, she prompted, "Well, what about them?"

"What about them!" Georgie said, as if a red barn couldn't be more obvious than the answer. "They're *boys*. And we're girls. And the faculty thinks any chance we have to get together there'll be some high old capers." She chuckled deep down in her throat. "And they're so right!"

"You mean like necking?"

Cathy knew it was a stupid thing to say, even before Georgie's laughter exploded around her, loud and harsh and unnerving.

"I love how you said that," Georgie said between gasps. "You sounded as innocent as a kindergartener, as though you'd never done it. What else is there to do with a boy?"

What else indeed? Cathy had spent the larger share of her life in the company of boys without once having run out of other things to do, but she didn't say it. There was such knowledge and sophistication in Georgie's tone that it did make a person feel "as innocent as a kindergartener"—and as babyish. But if that was all boys were good for here, they could stay on their side of the line for any interest Cathy had in them.

She tried to think of something to say that would not bring down the whole fire of Georgie's scorn on her, but a new voice, rising from the landing below, saved her the trouble.

"Boys, boys, boys!" it called on a rich, warm note that was not without a tinge of mockery. "I might have known that, whenever that kind of talk is floating around, I'd find Georgie Willis in the middle of it."

Footsteps, considerably lighter than Georgie's, ran up to join them, and the newcomer asked, "Hi, who's this?"

"She's Cathy Wheeler, the new girl in our room," Georgie told her and resumed the climb without bothering to complete the introductions. "How did you get here? We just had dinner, and I didn't see you in the dining room."

"By train and by taxi," the stranger answered, keeping pace with Cathy, who was a step behind Georgie. "I grabbed a hamburger downtown so I wouldn't have to check in until supper. I don't see how you can get so fat on the messes they serve here, Georgie." Ignoring the grunt she received in reply to this, she went on, turning toward Cathy, "How do you like it here? I suppose you just came this morning."

"Yes, with Miss Creel." Cathy's smile was so quick and easy that she realized she must have been forcing her other smiles a bit during the earlier part of the day. Whether it was the pleasing music of this girl's voice or the perfect timing of her accidental championship, she didn't know, but she was attracted to her as she hadn't been to Georgie. She was almost sure this was Francie Adams at last. "Georgie is still showing me around."

"And telling her about everything," Georgie added as the trio reached the fourth floor and filed into their room.

"Good for you, Georgie!" the latest arrival said.

"That's very sweet and thoughtful of you, I'm sure." She let her suitcase hit the floor with a bang, but her smooth, half-mocking tone didn't change. "One of these days they'll be giving you a medal."

Georgie did not answer. She became extremely busy, jerking open drawers in a bureau across the room, rattling through their contents and slamming them shut. The other girl began opening drawers, too, but quietly and methodically, as she transferred the contents of her suitcase into them. Cathy sensed a tension in the air that she could not understand beyond the fact that, somewhere along the line, she had missed a double meaning in what was being said. Locating her bed, she sank down on its hard edge, feeling embarrassed and uncomfortable and wishing she were home.

Nothing was said for what seemed an eternity. . . . She rubbed her fingers to and fro on the coarse, thin bedspread, pretending to admire the pattern which wasn't there until, to her immense relief, her coat slid off the bed onto the floor.

"Oh, darn!" she exclaimed, a shade too loudly, and jumped to her feet. "I forgot to put this old thing away."

"I'll hang it up for you if you want," the other girl said, snapping shut the clasps of her suitcase. "I have to stick mine in the closet now, too."

Before Cathy could thank her, Georgie cut in almost fiercely, "Let her hang up her own coat, Daisy. You know the rules."

Cathy, stooping to rescue the fallen coat, went numb for an instant, and then hot with confusion. This girl, this nice girl, was Daisy Brewer, the girl who stole things?

"I didn't know there were any rules against being

74

friendly," Daisy said. Her voice was icy cool in contrast to Georgie's snarl, but Cathy, who was hardly more than the width of a bed from her, caught the tiny thread of hurt that quivered through the words. "Why don't you go tattle to Her Majesty when she gets back, like you always do?"

Resentment boiled up in Cathy on Daisy's behalf. Georgie, about whom her feelings had been rather neutral until now, was nothing but a gossipy chatterbox, and, whether Daisy Brewer took things or not, it was pure spitefulness to be so pointedly nasty about it in front of a stranger. If a warning to Cathy was her aim, a simple introduction on the stairs would have served the purpose, without pain to anybody, but Georgie was apparently the type who bought her importance at other people's expense—by snatching them dramatically away from imaginary lines, for instance, and assuming a worldly-wise superiority in explaining why.

As Daisy rounded the foot of her own bed and started for the closet, Cathy impulsively held the coat out to her. "If you really don't mind—" She wished she'd had the nobility not to permit herself the thought, even fleetingly, that there was nothing in her pockets worth stealing, anyway.

"I'll hang it toward the front, where you won't have to hunt for it if you want it," Daisy said, exactly as if there had been no discussion of the matter at all. From the closet, she added, "There's a bag of popcorn on my bed, Cathy, the one next in line to yours on this wall. Help yourself. I suppose you can have some, too, Georgie, if you're not afraid of looking like a pig."

Georgie established her true character in Cathy's eyes, once and forever, by accepting the offered food without an instant's hesitation or the faintest sign of chagrin at being returned good for evil. By the munching sounds she made, she was using both hands to stuff a mouth that closed only to smack its lips.

Perhaps there was purpose in Georgie's haste, however, for the popcorn bag was scarcely emptied and tossed into the waste-basket when the other girls began arriving. Hope Cowley was first, trailing the odor of perfumed hand lotion across the room to her bed and declaring in gently querulous tones that one more step lugging that ghastly suitcase would be the death of her. Next came Ida Smith, a girl who sounded tall and thin, and who had a nervous laugh that reminded Cathy of the twitter of a flock of sparrows. Practically treading on Ida's heels, lumbered Emma Johnson, slow speaking and slow moving, and also slow thinking, for she had to have Cathy's presence brought to her attention three times by three different people and to be saved twice from falling over the extra bed before any of it appeared to register in her consciousness.

The last to make her entrance was Francie Adams. Cathy was wondering about her long delay and half inclined to believe that either Miss Creel had not seen right or else no such person actually existed, when a silvery laugh from down the hall shut off the chatter in the room like a switch.

Georgie shouted, "Francie!" and galloped out, to return puffing under the weight of two suitcases, which she knocked against Cathy's bed and then against the bureau in her eagerness to set them in the most convenient spot.

"Hi, everybody! I'm back to the old roost," said someone in the doorway to whom the silver laugh unmistakably belonged. "Here, Georgie, hang up my coat for me, will you? I'm dead. Simply dead."

"Sure, Francie. But wait a minute." Georgie grasped Cathy's right arm and dragged her from her seat on the bed, pushing her forward as if she were a piece of merchandise to be displayed to a favorite customer. "This is Cathy Wheeler. You remember, the new girl they told us would be here after Christmas?"

"Naturally I remember. Hello, Cathy. Welcome to 410."

A slender, cream-smooth hand pressed Cathy's and a delicate aura of lavender fragrance drifted through the air. Cathy was a little awed by the studied graciousness of the words and the elegant languor of the fingers that slipped free of hers. It was rather like receiving a favor from royalty, and her smile, although sincere enough, lacked the warmth Daisy's greeting had inspired.

"Thank you," she said, and retreated to her bed, knowing without being told that the interview was for the moment at an end.

Francie flung herself on her own bed, bouncing a creak of protest from it. "Girls, you'll never guess what I've been doing all day! And with whom! My train got in at nine this morning, and I've been bumming around downtown ever since. Miss Creel spotted me once, and I nearly died, but I waved sweetly at her, and she drove on by, smiling, so I'm positive she didn't notice *him*." Her feet hit the floor on the other side of the bed, and a suitcase grated on the bare floor as she pulled it closer. "That reminds me. I promised him I'd have my red sweater on for him at supper tonight, so I'd better do some fast unpacking."

Above the immediate chorus of shrill whispers and giggles of, "Who, Francie? Tell us who!" Daisy yawned and drawled, "Clancey, of course. Red's the only color he knows by name. Besides, I saw them together in the

Dirty Spoon when I was having a hamburger, but the romance was too thick in their booth for them to notice me. Lucky I don't have the babble bug or we'd be short a roommate tonight."

"Daisy Brewer, you wouldn't dare!" Francie snapped, then modified it with a slightly tarnished tinkle of her silver laugh. "But thanks, just the same." Wrenching a drawer open in the bureau, she changed the subject by exclaiming, "Who's been putting their things in these bottom drawers? Oh, Georgie, it's you. I can tell by the mess they're in."

"That's not my stuff," Georgie rasped gleefully. "That's Cathy's—our new roomie."

Cathy sat up straight, shame twisting her voice small. "Yes, those things are mine, I guess. Georgie told me I should use the bottom two drawers."

"Well, from the state of them, you'll surely fit in around here," Francie said, briskly closing them.

Cathy joined in the general laugh, but her face burned and her eyelids stung as though they had smoke in them. It was true that she didn't have much experience in the finer points of housekeeping. This was the first time she'd ever moved into a place by herself. It was even the first time she'd ever spent a night away from home without being in the charge of her parents or grandparents or one of her aunts—except for her hospital stay, of course. But then every least thing was done for her. Francie couldn't have hit her in a more vulnerable spot if she'd tried, and Cathy's defenses crumbled in on themselves like parched sand, leaving her too crushed to argue for herself or, much less, to resent her critic fully for the moment.

Five minutes later, the supper bell rang, and the incident was over, but, after the pupils were dismissed from the tables, Cathy found her way to the stairs by herself and hurried up to the room while the others were still milling in groups in the lower hall, talking to their friends. Room 410 was no problem to locate because it was the door immediately to the left of the stairway, and, once inside, the hiss of the radiator at the far end and a touch of her fingertips to the cold curve of the foot of her bed confirmed her sense of direction. Moving to the other side of the door, she dropped to her knees in front of the bureau and slid open the offending drawers.

Nothing was changed from the way she had arranged her things this morning. In the top one lay her pajamas, beside them a low pile of fresh underwear and, in the far corner, several pairs of clean socks rolled together in the balls her mother always made of them. The lower drawer held two sweaters, her brush and comb, a soap dish and, in a separate box, her toothbrush and a tube of tooth paste. Not only were the drawers too bare to be really untidy, but pajamas, underwear and sweaters all were laid in the same neat folds with which her mother had packed them into the suitcase. She wouldn't be ashamed to show them to anyone—or wouldn't have been, two hours ago.

Someone was coming up the stairs. Cathy pushed the drawers shut and got quickly to her feet, trying to look collected and serene.

"Oh, there you are, Cathy," Daisy said, pausing in the doorway. "I was wondering what became of you." She went on into the closet for a minute, and when she emerged, her tone was more serious. "Cathy, don't let Francie bother you. I know she hurt your feelings, and I told her what I thought of her for it, too. But she's got the idea that, because her folks have money, she's some kind of a queen around here. If she sees she can't make you jump when she snaps her fingers, she'll leave you alone after a while, though, so pay no attention to her."

"Thanks, Daisy." Cathy's smile was rather wan, but, again, it was real. "I'm not much of a jumper anyway."

It was a brave speech, but it did not count for much when bedtime brought everyone together again, and Georgie's giggled account of her foolish remark about the boys became the center of the lively after-lights conversation. Cathy hugged her knees under the bedclothes, her spirits writhing, as Hope Cowley's plaintive flute inquired:

"Cathy, how old *are* you?"

Cathy was taking no chances on being the youngest in the room. She knew Georgie was fifteen, and she suspected that some of the others, Francie especially, were that old or older, too, so she avoided a direct answer. "I'll be in the same English class as Francie."

"Really?" Francie asked. She was screwing the cover on a jar of hand cream she'd borrowed from Hope. "In the ninth grade class or the high school freshman? I'm taking both."

"But ninth grade is high school freshman," Cathy said, startled off her guard.

Daisy's matter-of-fact friendliness cut through the superior tinkle of Francie's laugh. "Not here it isn't. There's ninth grade, and then there's the first year of high school. You can ask for special permission to take them both at once, but otherwise this is a five-year high school. That's because a lot of the kids that are sent here can't see too well since there's something wrong with their brains."

"Why, Daisy!" protested Ida's sparrow twitter. "What a thing to say."

"Well, it's the truth," Daisy insisted, rustling herself into a better position for arguing in her bed. "And you know who they are as well as I do, Ida. All the classes here are geared for the speed of the slowest pupil, and they just made that new rule that, if you haven't graduated by the time you're twenty, you have to quit. This is a school for morons."

The current of interest swerved instantly from Cathy, and a full scale attack was launched on Daisy, who seemed quite capable of handling it.

Cathy lay stiff and straight, listening, hardly daring to stretch a toe for fear the movement would recall her to the minds of the other girls once more, and yearning for the hour when they would finally be talked out so that she could put an end to this miserable day by trying to sleep. The bed was narrow, the mattress hard, and there was a deep hollow in the middle of it that kept her from lying anywhere else on the surface. There was no privacy in the bedroom—not even for her clothes—and no food in the dining room that she would eat, unless she were starving. Instead of catching up to where she belonged in school, she was apparently losing a grade, wasting a year, and the only friend she had in the world was a girl supposed to be an outcast and a thief. And everything, every bit of it, was rising up against her when she had no eyes to help her fight back, while she was still new and shaky in a world of nothing but sounds and smells and touch. Never in her life had she felt so lonely and lost and deserted.

When at last Cathy risked rolling over to press her face into the pillow, she didn't even have the courage to let her homesickness trickle out in tears.

5

How CATHY lived to the end of that week . . . and through the next . . . and through the one after that without dying of sheer misery, was forever a mystery to her. Each day was drearier than the day before, and each night when the eternal whispered conversations in the dormitory faded to silence and she could fall asleep, she dreamed so regularly and so vividly that she was safe at home once more, that it was a fresh shock each morning to find herself still lying in the narrow iron cot, a hundred miles away.

If it had not been for the vision of the coming Saturday and Sunday that she clung to like a life preserver through the boundless sea of days that separated her from the train that would bear her homeward on Friday evenings, she was sure she would not have survived at all. At least, she wouldn't have wanted to survive. Yet even the precious weekends, the first few especially, were disappointing, for there was always the shadow of the Sunday night return to Burton lurking in the corner, and no amount of arguing or begging or tears could persuade her parents to remove it.

"You knew when you went with Miss Creel that the understanding was that you were to finish the school year at Burton," her father said again and again. "If you want to try public school here, you can next fall, but it's too late to make arrangements for that now. I'll look into this ninth grade and freshman business, so you won't be losing out on any of the work you have to have, but you decided on Burton yourself, and you'll simply have to stick to it until June. I'm sorry, but that's how it has to be." His voice sounded sympathetic— but very firm.

Sorry wasn't the word to describe *her* feelings! She was desperate, too desperate to believe that he couldn't work some kind of miracle with the school authorities if he just realized how wretched she was, but her remnant of hope was crushed by her mother without warning one Sunday afternoon as her dread of having to leave threatened to overflow into the suitcase they were packing.

"If you are going to go to pieces like this every Sunday, Cathy, I'm afraid it might be better if we didn't let you come home for weekends at all any more. Bad as Burton is, you don't seem to be a bit happier here, and it's upsetting for everyone to be put through this sort of thing week after week. I'd hate to say you couldn't come home until Easter, but, unless you can try to be a little pleasanter to have around—"

In shocked silence, Cathy admitted her defeat. Her own family had turned against her and was standing by to be certain the key was twisted in the prison lock. She felt kin to the pitiful man in the iron mask of *The Three Musketeers,* the poor young prince who was doomed to be shut up within grim walls forever because his presence in the world was a discomfort to his family.

Cathy was sitting in class the next morning, poking her Braille stylus into the tips of her fingers for want of something more constructive to do, when a faint whiff of ether—it might have been glue or nail polish —came to her on a current of air from the hall, and with it came the explanation. This was all a dream, a nightmare she was having; none of it was true. In reality, she was probably still on the operating table in the hospital, and presently she would be waking up to find her mother and father beside her and Dr. Kruger telling her that the operation was a glorious success and that she was going to be able to see better than ever.

The more she revolved the idea in her head, the more logical it became. Where else but in a dream would she, Catherine Elizabeth Wheeler, whose life had always been smooth and ordinary, who had always been able to see nearly as well as anyone else, to read and to draw and to be thrilled by beautiful sights, whose future as an artist was already planned—where else but in a dream would she suddenly be struck blind? How, except in the grip of a horrible nightmare, could she be thrust into a bleak institution by her parents and left to die of homesickness where every day was as long as a week? Things like that didn't happen to real people. They couldn't be actually happening to her.

Like a voice heard in a dream, Miss Tate, the Braille teacher, was saying far off and monotonously, "Here is your paper, Cathy. Copy it over and pay attention to the grade two signs. Where did you ever get the notion that *bef* stood for *before?*"

The sheet of stiff Braille paper slid onto Cathy's

desk and under her fingers. She didn't answer because she didn't feel like making the effort, and, in a dream, it didn't matter anyway. Besides, she didn't like Miss Tate, who was elderly and blind and never had a pleasant word to say, and who smelled as if she'd been soaked in some sort of mentholated medication for years. . . . After a while, Cathy drew the paper closer and, fitting a new sheet into her slate, began languidly re-copying the spoiled exercise, but whether she got it right this time or not didn't matter either. Nothing mattered. Nothing that she said or didn't say. Nothing that she did or left undone. Nothing that might be said or done to her.

It was a strange sensation, this being asleep and being aware that you were. It was as if her body were just a robot, going mechanically through the motions of the day, while she herself was a tiny spark of intelligence, housed at a remote control panel in a protected corner of the robot's brain, peering out now and then for the sake of direction or to speak to someone such as Daisy, but mainly withdrawn into the padded snugness of a shock-proof world of her own.

The rest of that day slipped by without touching Cathy, almost unnoticed . . . and the next day as well . . . and the next . . . and the next, until their edges ran together like water colors, and she lost the desire even to keep count.

Perhaps it would have been different if there had been anything to occupy her mind, but the infrequent assignments were so small and the pace of the classes was so dragging it was seldom that tomorrow's homework could not be finished before the dismissal bell rang for today's class. The science course had promised something better, for it had a young and enthusiastic teacher and the room boasted a real skeleton which could be examined by curious pupils, but this class, too, was constantly bogging down because of somebody who could not remember what was said yesterday or could not figure out what was being explained for the tenth time today. Her Braille reading was still too labored to make the library attractive, and if she went into the fourth floor sitting room to play the talking book, Ida and Hope or some girls like them were bound to be there ahead of her, listening to a slushy love story and setting the needle back again and again to the part where the hero crushed the heroine in his arms to press burning lips to hers. It was easier to follow the course of least resistance, doing what must be done but no more, and lying on her bed between times, letting her mind go blank while the days drifted into weeks, and the weeks into a month, a month and a half, and on and on and on . . .

The whole year might have melted away from around Cathy as quietly as snow from around a hibernating bear, if Daisy had not become insistent that Cathy go to the basketball game with her one night.

"Come on, Cathy," she urged, clamping herself to the foot of the bed and rocking it to and fro on its casters. "There's nothing to do up here tonight. Nothing worth listening to on the radio."

"No, I don't want to," Cathy replied listlessly. She never did care for basketball, and what fun was there in sitting through a game she couldn't see? If it were anyone but Daisy asking her, she wouldn't even have bothered to hunt for an excuse. "The rest of the kids are going, aren't they? You'll have lots of company. I'm too tired, and it's too cold to walk over to the gym."

Georgie paused in a grunting attempt to zip herself

into the skirt she had borrowed from Emma. "Are you sure you don't mean you have something else planned for tonight? Something private? I know somebody who was hoping you would."

A flurry of "Who? Who?" and "Don't keep it a secret," erupted as excitedly as though everyone supposed Georgie was actually capable of not telling.

"Well, if you must know," Georgie said, putting all the drama into the revelation that it would take, "it's Earl Lee. He asked me this morning if our 'little red-headed roommate' was going with anybody back home, and if I thought she'd be interested in going with anybody here. He hasn't gone with a girl now for a year."

"Because there aren't any left that he hasn't gone with before," Daisy said.

Cathy made a languid production of folding her arms beneath her head. She was both surprised and annoyed by the spark of curiosity that was threatening to revive her attention. "Who is Earl Lee?"

"He's in our science class," Georgie informed her eagerly. "He's tall and thin, about nineteen. He sits in the row next to yours, two seats in front of you."

"The one who asks all those dumb questions?" Cathy laughed her disdain and, rolling over, sat up, angry at herself for having been roused so neatly from her comfortable indifference to everything. "If that's the only choice I have, I guess I'd as soon go to the basketball game."

Daisy clapped her on the shoulder, delighted. "That's the spirit. I left some stuff in the sitting room that I have to get, but I'll be right back, and then we'll go."

She ran off down the hall, and Cathy, still half unwilling, crossed the brief expanse of floor between the end of her bed and the bureau to get her comb. Francie was standing there, crackling a comb through her own hair with long, swift strokes that suggested its style was loose and flowing. She stepped aside barely far enough to allow Cathy's drawer to be opened a hand's breadth, but Cathy eased her hand in sidewise for the comb and, squatting on her heels, whipped order into her short, straight mop in complete silence. Since that first day, she had avoided saying anything to Francie that was not absolutely necessary, and few things were.

It came as something of a shock, therefore, when Francie said suddenly, "Would you mind a piece of advice, Cathy? We've all been noticing, and I think that someone ought to speak up for your own good."

Cathy warily returned the comb to its place and pretended to search for another object in the drawer. "I don't know whether I would mind or not," she answered carefully, although a flicker of intuition warned her as to what might be brewing.

Francie accepted the words as an invitation to continue. "Well, it's about the friends you choose here. You don't want to get too thick with anybody until you're sure she's the type person you honestly want for a friend. In a school like this, there is every kind, and you have to exercise a little judgment." She hesitated, but less from embarrassment at what she was saying, Cathy felt, than from a desire to produce her final statement as impressively as possible. "To put it bluntly, I wouldn't be seen too many places with a girl who had a reputation like Daisy's, if I were you."

Cathy shut the drawer and stood up. She was not as tall as Francie, but the abrupt stiffness of her backbone gave a sense of towering. "No, I don't suppose you would." She was remembering how naturally Daisy had disregarded her chance to destroy Francie's reputation by reporting to the ever-suspicious authorities that stolen day Francie and her beloved Clancey had shared downtown. This was Francie's idea of gratitude.

Apparently, Francie got the message, for she edged away as Cathy walked by her, and the silver of her voice lost a degree of its usual coolness. "No, I wouldn't. And you're asking for big trouble unless you change your attitude pretty quick."

Cathy's blood was heating fast, but she had to swallow a giggle. The line was straight out of a Western, and the retort leaped off her tongue almost of itself. "Big trouble from whom?"

"You don't like it here, do you?" challenged Georgie from her bed, which was beside Francie's.

"Not much," Cathy answered, reminding herself that this was all part of the dream, and that here, if anywhere, she might as well enjoy the luxury of being frank.

"Well, I'd advise you to start liking it," Francie said. "You've got at least four more years here before you graduate, and I can promise you plenty of misery if you keep on being so independent and don't start acting and thinking like everyone else. You're not such a lot better than the rest of us."

"Who said I was?" Cathy asked. She took pains to adjust the hang of her skirt, centering the zipper over her left hip exactly where it belonged. "And who said I was coming back here after June? I'm going to be in Wilson High School at home this fall."

If she had thrown a lighted firecracker into the middle of the room, the effect couldn't have been more explosive.

"You mean you really can go to the regular high school if you want to? And you'll be living at home?"

Hope made no effort to hide her envy. "Gee, I wish my folks would move to the city."

Ida switched off her little radio, on which she was forever hunting for romantic music and seldom finding it. "How are you going to do your lessons in a public school? If you want to take notes, you'll have to use Braille, right in front of everybody. I'd die of shame if any outsiders saw me reading a Braille book. Even on the train I carry a print book and make believe I'm reading it so that nobody looking will think I'm queer."

"I wouldn't go to a public school," said Emma ponderously. "They're mean to blind kids. They laugh at you and play jokes, and the teachers flunk you. They're all mean."

"I spent a day in my sister's high school once." Georgie giggled reminiscently. "We were walking between classes, and my sister's boy friend raced out of a classroom, wrapped his arms around me, kissed me, shoved a piece of candy in my hand and raced off to his next class. I don't know how they get any studying done in those schools."

Francie alone refrained from commenting, but her silence was hardly noticed in the storm of discussion that was still raging in the room when Cathy and Daisy descended the stairs on their way to the gym building.

The basketball game was no more of a thrill than Cathy had expected it would be, but it was a relief to shout at top volume with the others and let some of the pent-up steam out of her system. Afterward, she and Daisy pooled their change to buy themselves a giant, twenty-five-cent bag of popcorn and, on Daisy's suggestion, headed for the seclusion of the deserted English room to eat and talk.

"Say, what was the fuss about upstairs?" Daisy asked,

snapping on the lights. "I heard the tag end of it. Are you honest-to-goodness going to your home-town high school next fall, instead of here?"

Cathy nodded, tucking a leg under herself as she settled into one of the front desks. "I almost went this semester, but Miss Creel talked me into trying this place first, and now my folks say I have to stay here until June. But they've promised they'll see to it that I get back with my regular class if I want to, and I want to."

"Lucky you!" Daisy sighed. "I'd take off from here in a minute if there was any place else I could go."

Cathy's fingers closed on the popcorn bag Daisy nudged into them, but she didn't dive in for a handful at once, although popcorn and carmel corn and pretzels and potato chips and the other like products that the snack counter sold were the mainstay of her diet these days. "But you live in a fairly large town, don't you? And your eyes are good enough to read print, especially if you have a magnifying glass. Why do you have to stay here if you don't like it?"

"Oh, I tried going to our school at home for a year, but it didn't work out." Daisy scuffed a foot back and forth beneath the desk at which she was sitting. "We have a pretty big family, and my dad doesn't earn an awful lot, and sometimes we don't get along together too well. It's easier on him if the State is supporting at least me—and then something went wrong at the school, too, and— Well, it just didn't work out."

Cathy yearned to ask what it was that went wrong, but she lacked the courage and the thick-skulled bluntness to do it—in case there were some grains of truth in the tales Georgie and Francie spread. She had been at Burton now more than two months, without a lock or a key or a secret hiding place to her name, and, so far, not as much as the lint from her sweaters had turned up missing among her things. But the whispers and hints about thefts, and the occasional tiny digs that Daisy suffered undisputed, were hard to brush away absolutely, once they had registered themselves in a person's mind. Maybe it was true that Daisy stole things, but maybe she couldn't help doing it. There were such people. Kleptomaniacs they were called. Cathy remembered reading an article about them in one of her father's magazines, and later she'd seen a television play in which a sweet, lovely woman started shoplifting things she didn't even want because she was lonely for her busy husband and grieving for her dead baby. Of course, Daisy had no husband or babies, dead or alive, but her home didn't sound like a much happier place than Burton, and certainly Francie and the girls who paddled in her wake like a bunch of ducklings playing follow-the-leader—which was practically every girl from the sixth grade up—were as good as a guarantee that Daisy must be lonely.

Cathy chewed on a rubbery kernel of popcorn. "What are you going to do after you graduate from here? Have you thought?"

"Marry the first nice, rich guy that asks me and settle down to making him the best home he ever saw." Daisy said it so promptly that it was plain she'd given the question thought before this. Reaching into the popcorn bag for another handful, she added, "I know who he'll be, too—or I hope I do. He lives near me, and we've talked about it plenty of times. He's not millionaire rich or anything like that, but he'll be a junior partner in his dad's store when he's through school, and he's the nicest guy I ever met. If he still likes me as much after I graduate from here as he does now, it's all set."

Cathy hitched herself around on the seat to face her companion more fully, thrilled and a trifle awed. She knew Daisy to be a year older than she was, but none of her school acquaintances either here or at home, regardless of their age, had ever spoken of marriage as though it were so near to being an accomplished fact. And what an ideal solution to Daisy's problems!

"Daisy, how wonderful for you! Of course he'll like you as much then—even more, probably. How can he help it?"

To Cathy's astonishment, Daisy leaned over and hugged her. "You're a goofy little kid, do you know? Sometimes you act like you're too young and innocent to understand anything, and sometimes like you just don't give a busted shoelace. Francie and Georgie and half the other kids say they can't make you out. But that's because you've really got more on the ball than any of them, and they're jealous."

Cathy ducked her head, aglow with pleasure but uncomfortable, too. "Thanks." She couldn't make her own self out, so it wasn't exactly fair to blame Francie on that score, but neither was she eager to pursue the subject for greater enlightenment tonight.

"Oh, listen!" she exclaimed, glad of an excuse to switch the conversation to a less personal track. "Somebody's typing in the typing room. Who'd be down there now?"

"Ida, I'll bet," Daisy answered, her voice sinking to a lower pitch. She went tiptoeing to the door to see, the faint, protesting creaks of the floor boards fading momentarily into the hall and as quickly returning.

"It's Ida, all by herself. Writing another letter to Roy Rogers, I suppose."

"To whom?" Cathy would never have suspected twittery, fluttery Ida of writing fan mail to a cowboy star—or venturing to write fan mail to anyone, for that matter.

"Roy Rogers," Daisy repeated carelessly, sitting on the corner of Cathy's desk and crackling the bag in search of a few remaining kernels. "Poor kid, she's been doing it for years. In a couple of days, she'll show up after mail delivery with a fat Braille answer from him."

"Roy Rogers writes Braille letters regularly to Ida?" Cathy licked grains of salt from her finger tips, uncertain whether to be incredulous or impressed.

Daisy's chuckle gave her the clue, although there was none of the sneer in it that Georgie or Francie would have felt necessary to point up the information. "Nobody's ever seen the Braille letters but Ida—up close enough to read, that is. She used to read parts aloud to us, mostly stuff like how glad he was to hear she was over her cold, and how he was hoping she'd have no trouble with her exams, and how he thought her new boy friend sounded great, and fatherly type things like that—but Georgie got funny one night and tried to grab a page away from her, claiming it was nothing but an old arithmetic paper. Well, Ida went into such hysterics that we had to call in the house mother. Lucky for Georgie that Ida doesn't have any family except a great-aunt who's mostly too sick to care much what happens here, or there might have been worse trouble. Folks like Francie's, for instance, barge in and raise the roof in the principal's office if their darling child ever stubs her toe on a chair some naughty pupil forgot to set just so." Daisy crumpled the bag and tossed it into the waste basket at the side of the room, where it landed with a soft plop. "There's some hard kernels for Creepy Creel when she walks in here tomorrow morning. Shall we head for upstairs?"

As if in answer, the bell jangled through the building, warning that there were only fifteen minutes left before lights-out. Cathy reluctantly agreed that they'd better not linger, although it meant dropping the most intriguing conversation she'd known since she was at Burton.

Nevertheless, she was not sorry to climb into bed, between the sheets that smelled of disinfectant, and to stretch herself in the hard-sided trough of the mattress. The evening had showered food for thought on her in such a variety of morsels that she needed a quiet space to sort and examine them. She needed a quiet space, too, for pulling the knowledge of her dream life around her again, for her awareness of it had receded to a dangerous distance in the past two or three hours.

But Francie had other ideas. Lights-out was always the signal in 410 for the launching of a prolonged and most confidential, discussion of boys, and tonight she had a fresh chapter to add to the worn collection of confessions and speculations. Not merely had she managed to sit beside her darling Clancey at the basketball game, but afterwards they had sneaked outside for a forbidden quarter hour in the dark, and she was determined to share or, as Cathy felt, to gloat over her triumph in minute detail.

"He's so solid and muscular," she was murmuring in a half whisper when Hope's little Swiss clock chimed eleven-thirty. "I go positively limp in a pair of strong arms, and his are the strongest I've ever been in. The whole faculty could have been standing there tonight watching us, and I wouldn't have known. And if that weren't enough, just as we were about to go in, he bent down and kissed me and *nibbled my ear!*"

From the ecstatic gasp that rose on all sides, Cathy gathered that ear nibbling was an extreme among romantic thrills, regardless of how unappetizing a practice it might appear to the uninitiated. Hunching herself lower under the blanket, she wondered what sort of thrill it was and how it would seem to go positively limp in strong arms. She couldn't imagine wanting to kiss Pete, let alone caring to have him hug her. A couple of years ago they had seen a movie together where a solid and muscular young pirate received a bite in the shoulder from the heroine when he wrestled her up against a wall to get a kiss, and she and Pete had re-enacted the struggle a dozen times, taking turns being the masterful pirate, but, by unspoken accord, they'd omitted both the bite and the kiss from the scene. Yet, from the way they talked and the tales they told, nearly every girl in 410—including stolid Emma—would risk any penalty the school could impose for such an opportunity, and the school had plenty to impose. Maybe it was true that she, Cathy, was too young and innocent to understand, for until she came to Burton, she'd given scarcely a thought to these matters, but, like the repeated slurs on Daisy's character, this enthusiastic flow of revelations lodged strange flecks and particles in her mind that had a tendency to stick.

Cathy fell asleep still wondering, and in the morning, although she reminded herself often and sternly that she was drifting in a dream that would vanish to nothing soon, the old, cushioning indifference couldn't pad her from a ripple of expectancy as she entered the science class and walked by the desk in the next row and two seats ahead of hers. Earl Lee, she discovered, was not difficult to distingush from the other boys, once his existence had been brought to your attention, for he had a deep, slow voice that rumbled his words along like the cars of a freight train, and he let no statement of the teacher pass without a question or some dull joke on it. Dumb, was her verdict, stupid, oxy dumb, as might have been foreseen of a nineteen-year-old fellow bogged down in ninth-grade science the same as Emma, who was eighteen, but he was worse than Emma because she laid no claim to being a wit. All the same, it was rather flattering to be singled from among the other girls, even by a stupe, and Cathy bestowed a small but not altogether chilling smile on him when he jostled her in the doorway at the end of class and said, "Hi, there, Red."

It was a short-lived smile, though, for a quite different voice sprang at her from across the hall. "Catherine! If you have a free period now, I wish you would come into my room."

Cathy's heart flipped over and sank. "Yes, Miss Creel," she said, and instantly her conscience began a churning review of her recent actions, trying to discover what it was she must have done wrong.

Miss Creel did not leave her long in suspense. Barely waiting for Cathy to step beyond the threshold, she closed the door, and said, "Sit at any of the desks. I want to have a serious talk with you about the reports I've been hearing about you lately. They aren't very pleasant, and I'm disappointed in you. I understand you don't think you are very happy here."

Cathy placed her folder of papers and her slate on the desk she'd used last night and slid onto the seat.

There didn't seem to be much point in hunting for a reply, because it sounded like just the preamble to what was to come.

Miss Creel trundled her desk chair around in front of her own desk, and a series of squeaks told that she was seating herself on it. "You know, Catherine, you aren't the first person on earth to suffer from homesickness. We've had youngsters here who actually had to have the services of a doctor because they were so homesick, but they cured themselves by putting forth an effort to adjust. There is Danny Holtz, for example, a boy who graduated last year as valedictorian of his class. He came here newly healed from a hunting accident that blinded him for life, but he went right to work learning the buildings and the grounds and how to get from place to place by himself. He didn't waste his time being dissatisfied and looking for sympathy as you are doing."

Cathy rolled the upper corner of her folder to and fro between her thumb and forefinger. Danny's feat didn't strike her as a wondrous accomplishment. She'd learned the buildings, too, inside of a week, and how to get where her class schedule required her to be, and she'd done it without particularly trying, either. What did weaken her knees was Miss Creel's method of point-blank attack, which caught her unprepared for defense while it whip-stung her resentment. "I'm not looking for sympathy," she said a shade above a whisper, and mentally added that, in any case, she would not be looking for it here.

"Then I wish you would tell me what you are looking for," Miss Creel suggested coldly. "Certainly you can't deny that you are dissatisfied. I've suspected from the beginning that you were too spoiled and obstinate a little girl to be otherwise, but, since that was your problem, I didn't say anything. Now it appears that you are becoming arrogant as well and disturbing those who have to live with you by behaving as though you were a law unto yourself and not subject to the limitations of common mortals."

Cathy sat motionless, stunned beyond the power of indignation. She couldn't conceive of what she had done to merit this, and she was far more at a loss as to how to respond. Name-calling among people her own age or younger was nothing to be astonished at, but such tactics from a grown woman and a teacher were something new in her experience.

"What do you mean?" she managed when she thought she could trust her voice not to shake.

"I am quite sure you know that better than I do. For one thing, you've deliberately slighted the advice and warnings of those older and wiser than you and have chosen for your special friend the least desirable girl on your floor."

Cathy jerked her head up. Daisy again! If they hadn't been attracted to each other from the start, this perpetual harping on the subject would have driven them to be friends anyway. "I chose the nicest girl I've met here," she said quietly.

"I wish I could believe that, for her sake." A click of Miss Creel's tongue dismissed the possibility. "It's fairly obvious to me, however, that your interest in Daisy Brewer bears the same stamp as your boasts about leaving Burton and graduating from a public school. You didn't measure up to the standards of our established leaders, so you're bidding for the importance you want by flaunting yourself as a bold nonconformist."

The corner of Cathy's folder was disintegrating into

shaggy bits of paper fuzz. She should have guessed that she owed this interview to the offices of either tale-peddling Georgie or Francie, the established leader. Doggedly she said, "I wasn't boasting. I am going to high school at home, starting next fall. Ask my parents if you don't think it's the truth."

Miss Creel permitted herself a dry cough of a laugh. "If I had fifty dollars for every boy or girl who ever sat where you are sitting and told me he or she was going to enter public school, and if I had another fifty dollars for every one of them who sat here again within three or four months and admitted he'd made a horrible mistake, I would be rich enough to retire. You have no idea what you would be letting yourself in for if you tried competing with sighted people. It's because the public schools are so difficult that institutions for the blind are necessary."

"I'm not afraid." Cathy was aware that her under lip was beginning to push forward in a sullen bulge that might justify Miss Creel's charge of obstinacy, but she was beyond caring. And perhaps she was obstinate—if not being obstinate meant she would be argued into spending the rest of her days at Burton! "I've been going to public school all my life."

"Not as a blind pupil," Miss Creel said, sounding quite as obstinate herself. "You'll be singled out and watched in everything you do as if you were a freak. Half of your classmates will snicker behind your back because you are different, and the other half will embarrass you by feeling sorry for you. Your teacher will pity you, too, and give you high grades, whether you work or not, or else they will resent the extra work you'll cause them, and either pick on you in class or ignore you completely. A few of our people who transferred to sighted schools were able to fight themselves through to graduation, but a very few, and they had mental qualities that would have made them outstanding anywhere. Also, they were especially well adjusted to their handicap, whereas I haven't seen any signs of your adjusting to it at all."

Precisely what was supposed to be involved in *adjusting,* no one ever troubled to explain, but drawing a deep breath, Cathy said, "I'll do it better in a sighted school, because I'll like it better there."

"Will you indeed?" Miss Creel's chair squeaked sharply. "I'm not going to waste reason on a stone wall, but don't you forget, young lady, that Burton doesn't need your recommendation. It's our records and reports on you that your school will want to see before they open their doors to you."

A premonition crept over Cathy. "But I haven't broken any rules. And I've done all the work that was assigned."

"Really? Why don't we just have a look at what you've been doing?" There was another squeak from the chair, and Miss Creel's flat shoes thumped to the other side of the desk, where she rustled through a quantity of papers for a minute. "Here we are: the test on de Maupassant's *The Necklace* your class took last Monday. I graded the papers this morning. If they weren't in alphabetical order, yours would still be at the bottom of the pile."

Cathy stretched her hand to receive the paper as the flat shoes thumped toward her. She couldn't believe there was much on it to worry about, for she had never failed an English test in her life, and this test, on one short story and an interesting story at that, had been unusually simple. Her fingers sought for the Braille tag she knew would be clipped at the top of the typed sheet. It said—she had to read it twice to be sure, and then to say it aloud—"Fifty-five."

"The lowest grade in the class," Miss Creel said. "In fact, the only failure. You would have had a perfect paper, too, but I had to take off fifteen points for each misspelled word, and you didn't have any of the characters spelled right."

"But they were all big French names," Cathy gasped. "I never studied French. The story was on a talking book record, and I didn't ever see them, but I spelled them the way I thought they sounded."

"You spelled them incorrectly, however. That is what counts."

The gross unfairness of it stung Cathy's face like a slap. She doubted that she could be hearing right. "What about the rest of the class? Some of them must have been just as wrong."

"The rest of the class consists of people working sincerely to graduate from Burton. A teacher has a duty to consider the character of her pupils, as well as their scholastic ability, and in my opinion, Catherine, you are an incipient rebel, who must be dealt with accordingly. I hope that a word to the wise will prove sufficient." Miss Creel returned to her desk and wheeled her chair around to its proper place behind it. "Unless you have something more to say, you are welcome to leave now and think over what we've discussed."

Cathy had nothing more to say. Stuffing the test paper inside her folder, she got to her feet and walked silently from the room. At the stairs, she turned automatically and started to climb. On the third landing, far above the activity of the school corridor on the first floor, she halted, a hand gripping the rail, to take stock of the "discussion" and of herself.

Her knees were shaky from the tension she'd been under and from her helplessness at the injustice of it all. An incipient rebel, was she? She, who had always regarded herself as somewhat of a coward when it came to breaking rules or defying authority, no matter what the occasion.

Her hands were damp, and her heart was jumping against the walls of her throat, but already her mouth was a tight, thin line of resolution. June was an eternity away, but nobody and nothing was going to cheat or scare her into staying at Burton a minute beyond the end of this semester. If it was a rebel they wanted, a rebel they would have. The worst they could do would be to expel her—and what punishment could be less painful? From now on, she would do as she pleased, let them do as they would about it.

Giving her sweater a straightening tug, she twitched her shoulders and went on up the stairs to find Georgie and tell her to flash the green light to Earl Lee.

6

THERE WERE two doors to the English room. One opened onto the first floor corridor that ran the length of the building and was the highway to all the classrooms. The other was at the side of the room, and opened beneath the stairway that led to the girls' dormitories. There was another stairway in that same area which descended to the mysterious regions of boilers and furnaces and janitors' rooms in the basement, but that was of no special concern to Cathy.

She dropped her paper and slate on a desk near the second door and, after making sure that both doors were securely shut, went to the range of shelves where the score or more of enormous volumes of the Braille dictionary were stored. Selecting the volume containing the *M*'s, she lugged it back to the desk and sat down to do the word assignment for tomorrow. Whatever Burton's record might show in regard to her "adjustment," she was determined there should be no more excuse, justified or otherwise, for reporting that she was unwilling to do her work or was incapable of doing it.

Of course, she could have done this dictionary assignment this afternoon, during her study period, if she'd wanted to, but she rather liked the deserted air that settled on the first floor in the evenings a short while after supper. It was pleasant to feel solitary and private sometimes, and there were precious few places or moments here for achieving that. Besides, the homework gave her a reason for being in the English room at this hour of the evening, in case anyone should drop by uninvited. Not that it mattered to her whether she were caught without an adequate explanation, but it wouldn't be quite fair to Earl, who was squeamish about that sort of thing.

It was three weeks to the day since Miss Creel had delivered her "word to the wise." During these past fourteen days, Earl Lee had become practically a fixture in Cathy's life. He never failed to be waiting outside science class for her every day or to linger for a word with her afterward. No morning or afternoon went by without someone's smuggling a note from him into her folder. When she and Daisy ventured out of doors for a stroll, he was bound to appear between them on the block-long stretch of walk that was hidden from the school windows by the kitchens, and the afternoon she and Daisy checked out of the dining room to treat themselves to a hamburger supper downtown, they'd hardly chosen a seat before his deep drawl greeted them and he slid into the booth beside her. Daisy wasn't too fond of him. In fact, she called him pest and oaf to his face, but he wasn't easy to offend, and it was Daisy who had delivered the message that brought Cathy downstairs tonight. If nothing interfered, this would be their first meeting really alone.

She couldn't help a flutter of excitement as she paged

through the dictionary volume on the trail of *miscellaneous*. According to the grapevine, Earl was among the school's foremost "great lovers." Maybe tonight she would find out what she had been missing by being a tomboy for so many years.

Yet the cautious click of the latch and the muffled groan of the side door as it slowly opened robbed her of a share of her bravado. Why couldn't he have given her a little more time by herself? She stiffened and bent lower over her Braille slate, pretending that the dots she was punching kept her from hearing the footsteps entering the room.

"Hi there, Angel," Earl rumbled above her. That was his special name for her. He almost never said Cathy. "Don't I get even a smile?"

He tried to shut the book, but she slapped her hand onto it. "No, leave it."

"It's in the way," he said significantly. "You can flip it open again if someone comes."

She pressed her hand flatter. "I want to finish this first. We only had five words for tomorrow, and I might as well do them all, now that I'm started."

He spread his hand on hers and squeezed it hard, but when she wouldn't respond, he let her go ahead and look up the other four words. She took as long about it as possible, copying the definitions with a deliberation and care that would have wrung approval from sour Miss Tate, the Braille teacher. For no good reason, she was uncomfortable and on the verge of being angry. It was as if her earlier excitement had escaped through the door upon Earl's arrival.

Five words couldn't be made to occupy her forever, though, and finally she allowed him to slam the book shut.

"Now I'm putting this thing back on the shelf where it belongs," he declared.

Cathy sprang up. The desk had a bare and unprotected feeling without the huge, thick volume covering it. "No, don't," she said, following him quickly. "We had better leave it out. What will you do if anybody comes?"

"*Shh!* Not so loud," he warned in a half whisper and shoved the book into place among the others. "If we stand right here, we can be hunting for a book if somebody wants to snoop." He sidled closer and put an arm around her. "Any more problems?"

Cathy hesitated. "No, I guess not."

She yielded to the pressure of his arm, scolding herself for not being more eager. Certainly he was tall and muscular enough to suit 410's requirements. Her cheek bone was no higher than his shoulder, and her own shoulders nearly met in the front from the strength of his hug.

She waited for the thrill Francie had described so often, but, instead, she was aware of tiny details Francie hadn't ever mentioned, such as the sharp edge of a chipped shirt button digging into her chin, the protesting twinge of her backbone at being forced to an unnatural curve, the moist unpleasantness of hot breath puffing in her ear. Also, he smelled overwhelmingly of peppermint, which he had apparently chewed in hopes of disguising the almost as strong odor of the onions he had consumed at supper. She had to turn her face away or be suffocated.

"Hey! What's the trouble?" he objected, trying to tighten his hold on her.

"Did—did you hear someone?" she panted and, wi⸱

an emphatic push, struggled free of him. "There! Do you hear?"

"*Shhh!*" he implored. "Keep your voice down." Already he was at the side door, prepared to duck out at the slightest indication that the other was about to open.

What a noble creature he was, Cathy thought in a rush of scorn. He considered himself so masculine and irresistibly masterful, but, at the merest whisper of danger, he wilted like a scared bunny. What his masterfulness amounted to was sneaking around corners and behind trees, crawling out of the woodwork to strut like a rooster when he was sure some girl had cleared the coast for him and instantly deserting the ship with all on board if anyone said boo. A fast thinker might have told her he was anxious only to protect her by not staying for them to be caught together, but she doubted that Earl knew much about any kind of thinking, let alone fast.

Cathy walked to the desk that held her writing materials and sat down without deigning to act for a second as though she really believed in the spy she'd invented. Experience had taught her that Burton's unwritten law was, "Every man for himself," but there were those who at least had the gumption not to be craven in their obedience to it.

After a minute, Earl released his grip on the doorknob, letting the latch click into place, and tiptoed back to her side. "False alarm, I guess," he said and made a gurgling sort of chuckle, as if he were conscious of having appeared a trifle foolish.

"I guess," she said coldly, running a forefinger along the Brailled definitions before her.

"I better not stick around here too long, though. You never can tell." He eased himself onto the desk top and picked up her hand. "Gee, I wish we didn't have to wait until next year to get married."

"It is a shame," Cathy agreed and manufactured a polite laugh, for this was typical of Earl's idea of humor. She allowed him to keep her hand, because if she didn't, she would have no tale to pour into the expectant ears of 410 tonight, but she also wanted him to keep talking. "What's so special about next year?"

"Because I'll be twenty next year, and then I'm quitting this school."

"Without graduating?"

"Who needs to graduate? That's for guys who aren't smart enough to enjoy life unless a teacher's poking her nose in at the door every five minutes. I want to start living." He cuddled her hand in both of his, as though it were a baby in a cradle. "I'm going to have a cute little redheaded wife to snuggle up with whenever I please. That's enjoying life!"

A horrible suspicion slithered into her mind that perhaps he wasn't joking, but she tried to laugh it off. "Redheads are pretty expensive. How do you figure to pay for one if you don't even have a diploma to help you get a job?"

"Don't you worry about that. I'll take care of you. If you took a class in the trade department here, you'd see that I'm the best man they've got in the shop when it comes to caning chair seats or making brooms. I'm not the worst guy at piano tuning, either. There's plenty of work I can do."

"For a living?" She couldn't disguise her dismay, although she would have been the last ever to prophesy a future as a bank president or a nuclear physicist for him. Of course, chairs had to be made and brooms tied and pianos tuned by someone, she realized, but until now, she had regarded the rug and basket weaving and the other handicrafts taught in the school workshops as interesting and possibly profitable hobbies, rather than lifetime careers.

"Shh! Keep your voice down," Earl begged, but he took both her hands and patted them together between his, to show he wasn't angry, only cautious. "You've got to learn to be careful, Angel, or one of these days you'll have Creepy Creel walking in on us. But don't you worry. You have your old Uncle Earl to watch over you and see you stay out of trouble." On a prouder note, he added, "I guess I surprised you kind of, didn't I? You didn't know I had things figured out so well."

Cathy pulled her hands away and busied them in gathering her disarranged papers into a pile. This had gone too far. Talking about marriage as if it were almost an accomplished fact was wonderful and romantic when the girl involved was Daisy. But marriage as a fact for herself and with someone like this was something entirely and appallingly different. "You've left out one tiny little detail, though," she said firmly. "I plan to get my high-school diploma, and then I'm going to go on to college."

Whatever reaction she expected, it was not the hoot of laughter that all but rocked him off his perch on the desk in his efforts to hold it to a whisper. "Leave it to you to say the weird things!" he gasped when he could catch his breath. "I bet not another girl in this school would have been quick enough to make believe she won't get married because she's going to go to *college*. Two people with sense-of-humors like ours belong together. You can't fight it!"

Cathy frowned, her chin lifting. "I wasn't being funny. I mean it. I'm going to college. My father went,

110

and my mother went, and some day my brother will go, and when it's time, I'm going. What's so strange about that?"

"Listen," he said, still chuckling, "what do you think they spend so much time here teaching us trades for? To go to college? A guy from Burton went off to college a couple years ago, and he hasn't been heard from since. What do you think they put all you girls in the home ec classes for if they don't figure you'll be sweet little housewives as soon as you can get there? What do you want to be? A brain?" He leaned forward and clapped a big, warm hand on each of her shoulders. "Come on and be nice. I've got to blast off in a minute, and you haven't told me yet if you'll miss me during Easter vacation."

"I don't know," she said and tried unsuccessfully to shrug loose from him. She couldn't remember feeling less nice in her life. "Vacation doesn't start until next week Wednesday."

Undisturbed, he said, "I guess I'll just have to find out for myself."

The weight of his hands shifted, bringing him lower, and it flashed on her that he was about to kiss her. For a split second, excitement flickered up in her again. Then the fumes of peppermint and onions cut her breath short, and two wet, flabby lips planted themselves on hers.

"You'll miss me," he sighed. "Good night, my little red-headed angel."

He slid from the desk top and, without another word, exited dramatically through the side door. The moment it clicked shut behind him, she was out of the other and on her way upstairs. Once or twice she paused to wipe the back of her hand across her mouth, but her main desire was to be as far from the English room as fast as possible. She wasn't sick, but she almost wished she could be.

For the first time, 410 seemed like a haven. Dropping her slate and papers onto the foot of her bed as she entered, she reached for her wash cloth and towel on the chair rack, wanting to give her face and hands a thorough scrubbing. On an impulse, she postponed the face washing briefly, however, and, undressing quickly, hurried down the hall in bathrobe and slippers to steam herself from head to toe in the clean, soapy heat of a shower.

She returned to 410 just ahead of the lights-out bell, feeling much better, but the inner effects of her evening were not to be so readily rinsed away. When the nightly murmur of conversation drowsed into silence and there was nothing more to listen to but the irregular ping of the radiator and the rapid, delicate *tick-tick, tick-tick* heart beat of Hope's clock, she still lay wide awake, straining to think of something else besides the events that insisted on tramping through and through her mind. All the experiences the books and the movies and the girls proclaimed as most radiant, most rapturous in connection with one's first boyfriend—all of them were disappointing, horrid! If this was romance, she wanted no part of it ever again.

But, of course, it truly wasn't romance, and deep down, she admitted it. That was why, on top of everything else, her conscience was stinging her as well. From the very beginning, her opinion of Earl had been as low as Daisy's, but she'd smiled and giggled and deliberately led him on in order to spite Miss Creel. If she'd been disillusioned tonight, it was her fault as much as his. She had never dreamed, though, that he would become serious. Yet, now that it had happened, she couldn't deny that she was somewhat responsible. This seemed to mean that, much as she would enjoy pushing him off a ship in mid-ocean, she owed it to him to get herself out of this mess with no more damage to his feelings than was necessary. The question was, how?

She found no answer that night . . . and none was waiting to enlighten her when the rising bell clanged at six-thirty the next morning. Earl's vibrant whisper, "Hello, Angel," at the door of the science class made her stomach turn over, but, luckily, this was Friday, and she was safely on board the homebound train half an hour after her last class of the day.

Cathy yearned to discuss Earl with her mother, to get her viewpoint and her advice, but when the right moment came—when her father and Mark were beyond earshot, watching a sports film on television in the living room while she and her mother stood together at the kitchen sink, doing the dinner dishes—she didn't know how to begin. Suddenly, she was too embarrassed to mention a word on the subject, or maybe, if the truth were told, too ashamed, and the chance went by in silence. No other was offered before she was on the inevitable Sunday night train, headed once more for Burton and her unsolved problem.

Exactly how unsolved it was, she realized two hours later as the conductor helped her step down onto the Burton station platform. Usually he guided her across the tracks to one of the nearby taxis that were always on hand for the arrival of a train, but tonight he said, "Well, what do you know? It looks like somebody's here to meet you." Over her head, he asked, "Are you from the school?"

"Yes, sir," rumbled Earl's thick voice to the left of

her, and a big hand cupped possessively around her elbow. "I'll take care of her."

"See to it you do," the conductor said rather sternly. Apparently he had his doubts, for he added, "You're sure you'll be all right now, young lady?"

Cathy wanted to say no, but what good would it have done? So she nodded instead and thanked him, then let Earl propel her forward like a wheelbarrow until she judged her question would not be overheard. "What are you doing here?"

"Surprised?" he asked, too pleased with himself to notice the chill of her tone. "We can walk back to school. It's about eight blocks, along nice, quiet streets where nobody'll see us."

She shook his grasp from her elbow and set her feet squarely and flatly on the pavement. "It's after eight o'clock and I'm supposed to be checked in by nine," she declared. "Besides, it's too cold to walk that far."

"I'll keep you warm, Angel," he said, giving her a nudge that swayed her on her feet. "Don't you worry. And if you want a taxi, you'll have to find your own, because I'm not taking you anywhere near one."

Cathy set her chin firmly. She could find a taxi or as much assistance as she needed simply by raising her voice for it here on the sidewalk. But being a rebel inside the walls of the school was one thing; becoming a public spectacle was quite another. On the other hand, she'd had about as much of Earl Lee as she could swallow. She was sick and tired of him and everything he represented, and if he persisted in wishing himself on her at every turn and acting as if she were his personal property, she was going to forget that she owed him the slightest consideration.

"I said I don't want to walk," she repeated evenly.

"Please, Earl, let's get a taxi. If you can't afford it, I can pay for both of us, but I want a cab."

Earl chuckled, delighted. "Don't tell me my little Angel has a temper! Uncle Earl has something that'll smooth that out, though. But it won't be half the fun in a cab. You leave it to him to know what's best."

He tucked her arm into his, and she as quickly untucked it, shifting her suitcase to that hand and withdrawing a few steps. "I said no."

Nevertheless, an ignoble but practical corner of her mind was warning her not to carry her objections too far. If she angered him to the point where he would stalk off and leave her stranded here, she would be reduced to advertising her helplessness by asking favors from strangers. She cringed at the thought. And wouldn't that tickle his misplaced funnybone? A blind person could be made to pay dearly for the luxury of self-expression unless she were on familiar ground—a blind person who was dependent on the sight of other people. It was a humiliating admission, and it would not be easy to forgive him for forcing it on her.

Whose will would prove strongest, hers or Earl's, she never learned, for a car door thumped open a short distance from where she stood, and a man called, "Taxi, miss?"

She whirled to smile at him. "Yes, thank you."

"No!" Earl said loudly. "Go on. She's with me."

But she was already hurrying toward where she'd heard the man. Footsteps crunched on the snow that still crusted the edge of the sidewalk and the curbing. Then the driver's hand in its smooth leather glove closed on hers, and she was guided into the warmth of the taxi's back seat.

"What about him? The fellow? Is he coming?" the driver asked.

"No," she answered promptly, squirming her feet in between the seat and her suitcase. Now she was glad she had neglected to inform Earl that toting the luggage was a part of gentlemanly polish. "He would rather walk."

"O.K." The door slammed shut beside her, and in another second, the one beside the driver banged, too. The motor hummed—and Earl was left to draw what conclusions he chose from the romantic atmosphere of eight nice, quiet blocks in the chilly April night.

"I've picked you up before," the driver said cheerfully. "You want the blind school. Right?"

"Yes, thank you." Cathy folded her coat tighter around her knees and leaned back against the seat, wondering what he would have said if she had answered that there was nothing in this world she wanted less than the "blind school."

What a futile, senseless place it was! If your method of enduring it was to keep quietly to yourself and do your best to pretend it didn't exist, you were accused of ill adjustment and rebelliousness, but if you set yourself wilfully to defy the rules, you were more of a loser than ever, for the whole affair backfired on you, and nobody else paid the slightest heed. Judging by her actions, as though everything were understood and settled between them, Miss Creel did not even suspect what was going on under her nose, and, unless she walked in on a scene like that evening in the English room, she probably never would, for there was nobody to tell her. Hope and Ida were frankly overjoyed at having a new romance in their midst and all in favor of protection and preservation. Daisy had only scorn for talebearers of any sort, and Emma lived in a perpetually good-natured fog that threatened no one. Georgie's curiosity and ego were more than satisfied by Earl's asking her so often to carry notes for him, which she read en route, while Francie occupied a glass house too fragile for her to risk tossing stones any bigger than: "If I had no more hips than you do, Cathy, I'd be scared to wear a skirt without suspenders," or, "Why don't you get some frilly blouses, Cathy? You're not the sweater type, unless you want to be mistaken for a boy." As for Earl, well, they would have to catch him before he'd do any confessing that involved himself, and to do that kind of catching, Cathy imagined, they'd have to be track stars in the Olympics.

She dropped her hand to the plastic-covered seat to brace herself as the taxi rocked around a corner. What a blow this must be to Earl's pride, especially when he thought he was springing such a heart-throbbing surprise on her! Now that the incident was past and her temper beginning to cool, she was relieved the break had happened like this, so naturally and accidently. Likely he was calling her selfish and unreasonable and every other name in the book, with some justice, but that was good. It was fine.

"Tomorrow he'll expect me to apologize," she told herself, fumbling in her coat pocket for the fare as the cab slowed. "But I won't apologize. I'll go on being more and more unreasonable until it dawns on him that I'm not the sweet little angel he supposed, and that will be that."

That was not that, however, for there was a small flaw in her reckoning. Cathy had overestimated Earl's pride. He failed to meet her outside science class on Monday morning, but the following period, she had scarcely opened her folder in the library when Georgie jogged her shoulder and panted, "Hi," in her ear. A note was slipped into the crease of the folder pocket. It was in Earl's personal version of Braille, which, because he could read magnified print, he had never mastered beyond the unpunctuated ABC's, and, among those, he was perpetually confused as to which were I's and which were E's.

Once the code was deciphered, however, this message remained a puzzle:

my diarist angil pliasi gevi mi a chanci to ixplaen to you e creid mysilf to sliip last neght thenkeng e had lost you bue e know you ari too swiit to dicedi wethout lestineng to my sedi of it ferst   trustengly your iarl

Cathy read this through twice, her forehead wrinkling in a frown that was half bafflement and half disgust. What did he have to explain? Anybody with a quarter inch of spine ought to be fuming at how she had treated him last night, not begging humbly to be heard. Or was he trickier than she gave him credit for, and maneuvering to shift the blame for last night onto himself, so there would be no excuse for breaking up? Well, there was a time when her vanity might have been flattered by his caring that much, but that time was ancient history. Cried himself to sleep, indeed!

Cathy tore the note into halves and quarters and sixteenths and on with mathematical exactness until she had only a handful of confetti to shake into the wastebasket at the end of the table, but it was like trying to destroy the fairy tale tree that grew two chips in place of every one that was chopped out, for by noon she had two more misspelled notes, and at supper she found a third tucked under her plate. Each of them said the same: Earl was heartbroken, abject and positive she was too "swiit" not to let him "ixplaen."

She called to Georgie as the dismissal gong set chairs to scraping and feet to scuffing throughout the dining room. How Georgie managed to pass information safely from one side to the other of the no-man's-land separating the boys' section of the building from the girls', Cathy had no idea, but it was a talent that came in handy. Drawing her roommate aside, she said, "If you see you-know-who tonight, tell him I'm not as sweet as he thinks I am, and that nobody's explanations are going to change matters. You can tell him, too, that there's no use looking for me downstairs this evening, because I'll be busy until lights-out in 410."

"Good for you!" Georgie said. "Stick to your guns and let him suffer. I think you're perfectly right. There's a roll left on your plate. Mind if I take it?"

The last question was rhetorical, for Georgie made a practice of removing leftover tidbits from the tables she passed on her way to the dining room door after meals, but Cathy nodded, surprised and warmed by this unexpected championship. She was more astonished by the sympathy Hope and Ida poured on her when they found her alone in the fourth floor sitting room, hunting through the albums of talking books for something to amuse her while Daisy was off washing her hair at the opposite end of the hall.

"We won't talk about it if you'd rather not," Hope said in her soft, plaintive voice, "but we want you to know that we understand how you must be feeling. Just remember that it's better to have loved and lost than never to have loved at all."

"Yes," Ida chimed in. "At least you'll always know

what love is, now. I mean, at least you haven't missed *everything*."

Cathy shut the album of records she was examining and turned to face the pair. A suspicion was starting to grow in her that perhaps she had missed a good deal. Either that, or everybody was extraordinarily well informed on a matter she hadn't discussed even with Daisy. She decided against displaying her ignorance to these two, though, and, as soon as she could, left them to their speculations and went down the hall to the washroom, to learn what she could from Daisy.

"Here Cathy is now," Daisy said as the door opened. "Ask her yourself." Her voice was hollow, coming from the depths of the wash bowel. "Emma has a problem, Cathy."

"So have I," Cathy said. She paused a few steps beyond the door, listening for a hint of Emma's whereabouts, for Emma had a habit of moving with her hands held out limply in front of her, her fingers wobbling rather like the tentacles of a jellyfish. If you accidentally ran into them, they clung and crawled on you in a fashion Cathy much preferred to avoid. "What's your problem, Emma?"

"You aren't mad at Lorine, are you? She's scared of what you'll do to her," Emma said from near the shower stalls. "You won't do anything, will you, Cathy?"

"To Lorine Forbes?" Cathy vaguely knew the girl from having met her on the stairs once or twice. Lorine was fourteen, but she lived on the third floor, among her classmates of the sixth grade. "Why should I be mad at Lorine, or want to do anything to her?"

"Because of Earl," Emma said. "She didn't know you were going with Earl, or she wouldn't ever have sat with him. But she's scared you won't believe her."

120

"Sat with him where?" Cathy asked. "I wish somebody would kindly tell me what this is all about. Daisy?"

"Sat with him at the movies downtown. This Saturday and the one before." Daisy let the water surge down the drain. "Didn't anybody tell you?"

Cathy shook her head. "Everybody seems positive I know, including Earl. He's been apologizing all day without saying why."

"Serves him right." Daisy's deep chuckle shrank Earl Lee to proper insignificance. Her words began to spurt forth in jerks as she rubbed vigorously at her hair with a towel. "The first Saturday might have been that they just happened to get seats next to each other, but this Saturday it didn't just happen. I wasn't there, but the kids that were say he put on a better show than the movie. And then he had the nerve to tell me yesterday that it wasn't so bad, because he was pretending Lorine was you."

"Me!" Cathy sat on the edge of the bathtub to concentrate on a fitting name to call him. Lorine wasn't to blame. She followed the lead of anyone the slightest bit brighter than she was, and, according to Daisy, she had lived within the lovesick atmosphere of this institution from the age of five. But for him to pretend—and by pretending, to imply—that she, Cathy, would be that cheap and that public! . . . And here she was, wracking her brain for a means of saving his face for him because she thought it was the honorable thing to do. Contempt, indignation and fury swirled in her, but, suddenly, she was choked by a bubble of laughter. It was too ridiculous to take seriously. He wasn't worth the effort.

"Emma," she said, gulping down a giggle, "you tell Lorine for me that, instead of being mad, I'm grateful to her and glad for her. If she wants Earl, she is welcome to him, as a present from me, and I wish her all the luck in the world. She has my full, honest, complete, absolute blessing. And if you see Georgie—" She stopped, the cold of the tub seeping into the palms of her hands. "No, never mind. This is one note that will be delivered in person."

Emma stumbled off happily to reassure Lorine, and Cathy made a flying trip for paper, Braille slate and stylus. Returning to the washroom, where Daisy was pinning up her hair, she perched on the tub once more, and together she and Daisy composed the first and last note Earl Lee was ever to have from her. Revising and polishing kept them busy until almost bedtime, but Cathy declared it was the best fun she'd had since she had been at Burton. In fact, the two were so well pleased by the dramatic dignity they felt they had achieved in the final draft that Daisy regretted not having a bulletin board somewhere so they could post it for the edification of the entire school. It read:

Dear Earl, No excuse or explanation can change the facts. You must realize that it would be impossible for me to trust you again. Therefore I think it will be less painful to both of us if we face the truth immediately and consider our relationship is terminated. Perhaps this will serve as a lesson to each of us, and we will be wiser in the future. C. W.

Cathy agreed that it was casting pearls before swine to waste such a piece of literature on Earl, especially the parts about terminating their relationship and being wiser in the future, but that did not dim a single iota of her joy in "casting" the note as she brushed by his science desk the next morning, at the close of class. "Good-by, Earl," she said firmly, in a voice that carried to anyone who might remain in the room, and, her head high, her skirt swishing, she walked on out into the hall. She was a hundred pounds lighter on her feet for being rid of him.

"Catherine." Miss Creel's voice bit through her satisfaction. "Will you come down to my room with me, please? I have something I want to read to you."

The hundred-pound weight returned to Cathy's shoulder upon the instant. This time she had no need to search her memory for the cause of the summons. She knew. Ten days ago, she would have been defiantly glad to be caught, but it was hard now, at the very moment when she'd scrapped her rebellion as an expensive mistake.

Miss Creel pulled the door shut after they had entered her room, and went straight to her desk. "By the way, Catherine, do you have that test paper of yours on *The Necklace?*"

"No," Cathy answered, "I think I left it at home." She hoped she didn't look scared, but her mouth was dryer than a former rebel's ought to be.

"You had no business taking that home. The test papers of my pupils are my property. They are meant to be confidential between myself and the individual. They're no concern of anyone outside this class."

"I'll bring it back after Easter. I only showed it to my parents."

"Yes," Miss Creel's tone underlined the word, "and you told a pretty story to explain it, too, I don't doubt. You did a fine job of upsetting them. However, before you congratulate yourself over much, I want to read you this. It is a copy of a letter I mailed your parents this morning."

Cathy drew in her breath. Here it came! She planted her feet a little farther apart and, resting her left hand on the corner of Miss Creel's desk, stood ready.

Miss Creel read:

"Dear Parents,

"We are sending a transcript of Catherine's credits to the principal of Wilson High School as directed by your Superintendent of Schools. I have also recommended in a letter that Catherine be started in the first year of senior high school. I trust this meets with your approval.

"If Catherine finds it is quite impossible for her to carry on satisfactorily, please recall the correspondence that we had in which I stipulated that, very definitely, Catherine could be transferred back to our school very soon after it became obvious that the task was too great for her. Frankly, I am fearful that her attending the public high school at this time is not going to work out very satisfactorily. However, I hope that I am wrong in my opinions.

"I will be very much interested in receiving any reports on Catherine's progress as she goes along.

"Very truly yours,"

"The letter is signed by me," Miss Creel concluded.

Cathy's in-drawn breath refused to be released. She was going back to public school! It wasn't a boast or a dream or an idle promise. It was the truth! Her cheeks were burning from the sneers flung at her capabilities, but a glow of another sort was pulsing outward from her heart. Her parents hadn't deserted her, in spite of what she'd thought. They were on her side, fighting for her—and winning! They just hadn't wanted her to be a weak quitter and back down too easily, once she had started something of her own choosing. They had been warned against this. Suddenly, with a flash of insight, she realized that holding to this had been as hard on her mother and father as it had been on her.

"Well?" Miss Creel prompted.

Cathy shifted her folder higher into the crook of her right arm. Her face was too hot to permit a smile, but she said, "Thank you."

"Don't thank me. All this is much against my better judgment, and it isn't settled yet. The transcript of credits we are sending the principal of Wilson High School lists what you will have *if* you complete the required work this semester. Whether you can accomplish that or not remains to be seen."

Cathy raised her head the fraction of a degree and fixed her eyes on Miss Creel as steadily as though they could actually see her. Tomorrow afternoon was the start of Easter vacation. There would be eleven beautiful, uninterrupted days at home. When school began once more, April would be gone, and there would be only May and half of June to live through. That was a long enough time to have to endure here, but it was not so long as the time that was already past, and even Miss Creel could not prevent the last day from coming eventually.

"I can do it," she said.

She wasn't afraid of Miss Creel any more. It was Miss Creel who was afraid. Miss Creel was a bully, who liked to crack a whip above little people and make them cower, but she was afraid because she had overstepped herself in the matter of the test paper, and she hadn't counted on Cathy's having allies to stand up for her or having the courage to call them in. You didn't have to be a rebel or a lawbreaker to pay your score with her. You simply had to be unafraid.

Miss Creel slapped the letter down onto her desk. "What is the good of trying to talk to you? You are the type who never can learn except by ramming your own head into stone walls. If I weren't looking forward to the pleasure of greeting you when you come limping in here some time around the middle of next year, I would be strongly tempted to wash my hands of your case completely, this very minute. Get on along to the library or wherever you belong during this period."

"Thank you, Miss Creel," Cathy said automatically, and did not wait for a second urging. Being unafraid and being comfortable were two different things.

She forgot the wastebasket that was placed just inside the door. Her foot struck it a glancing blow, and the big, barrel-shaped basket emitted a clang that sounded like a fire drill. She swooped to her knees to save it from toppling on its side and strewing papers across the floor, but her dignity was lost in the process.

"Of course, that is one problem you won't encounter at Wilson High School," Miss Creel said, without offering to help. "They'll have a student or someone to lead you from class to class, and probably to bring you to school and take you home. You'll have to leave when she wants to go and stay when she wants to stay, and no doubt you'll have to join the after-school clubs she wants to join, but you won't be bumping into things, if she's careful. You'll merely spend the rest of your life hanging from someone's arm like a bracelet. I suppose you have thought of that."

"Yes," Cathy answered. That wasn't quite true, for

she hadn't thought of it before, not consciously, anyway. Nevertheless, she knew suddenly what her solution would be. It must have been growing slowly in the back of her mind for a great while, for she wasn't really surprised by it, but perhaps it had taken that clash with Earl at the station Sunday night to jar it toward the front, where she could use it.

Getting to her feet, she reached for the door and, with her fingers securely curled about the knob, she put the idea into words for the first time. "I'm going to get a guide dog," she said and, stepping into the hall, shut Miss Creel's door firmly behind her.

7

As THE Wheeler family car slowed to round a curve, Mark bounced forward to hang over the front seat, breaking off short the monotonous hum that was one of his methods of whiling away the time on a trip. "Is that the school? That building ahead with all those trees?"

"It could be," his father replied. "We'll know when we get close enough to read the sign, if you can wait that long."

Cathy leaned forward, too, bumping elbows with Mark, who could never find room enough in the back seat to share it properly. "How far?" she asked eagerly. The warm wind, rushing through the open windows of the car, carried the chirping of crickets, the silver gurgle of blackbirds and the sweet smell of drying hay. "Is it pretty? Do you see anybody around?"

"It's very pretty," her mother answered from the front seat. "If that is the place. There's not a soul in sight, though."

"Not even a dog," Mark said, disappointed. "I wonder

what kind they'll give you, Cathy. A big, wrinkled-up boxer, do you think? They look fierce. Or a collie maybe? Or one of those tall, skinny greyhounds, like they have in races? That would get you places in a hurry."

Cathy pressed herself tighter against the seat in front of her. She did not answer, because she did not know. In the three months since she had announced to Miss Creel that she meant to get a guide dog, she had imagined herself holding proudly to the harness of practically every kind of noble dog she had ever heard of, but the man who came to interview her before she was accepted by the training school had said he couldn't promise what breed of dog would be given to her, only that it would be the animal the trainer thought to be best for her. She would have to wait and see.

Her parents had greeted the idea of a dog with approval—and without surprise. It was as if they had discussed the possibility between themselves already and were merely letting it ride until Cathy should suggest it herself. When they learned, through research at the library, that there were a number of training schools scattered around the country, they wrote to all for further information. Many did not like to take students younger than eighteen, but there were a few willing to make exceptions in the case of young people who were attending regular public schools and could show a real need for a dog. Finally, Cathy decided on a school in her own state, just eighty miles from home. The arrangements were made, the date was set, and now, on this first Sunday in August, the waiting was nearly over.

"That's it!" Mark yelped. "This is the place! See the sign, Daddy? There's the name right there!"

"I see," his father said. "But if you don't get your head out of the way of the mirror, I won't be able to see if it's safe to turn, and we'll have to go right on by."

Mark ducked back to his side of the rear seat, and Cathy dodged into hers. Excitement plumed up in her like a fountain as the car slackened speed and swung left onto a gravel drive that crunched and spattered under the wheel.

The descending spray of the fountain, however, fell on her spirits, wet and rather chill. It was barely more than six weeks ago that she had shaken the dust of Burton from her heels for what she hoped would be forever, regretting only her tearful parting with Daisy. Since then, it had been almost as if she had never been away from home, as if Burton were only a bad dream she did not have to think about and that she would not dream again. Yet here she was on the brink of entering another boarding school, to live among strangers, blind strangers who were probably little different from the self-centered, ever suspicious Burton blind. And this time she was to have not so much as one weekend of relief at home during her training session. For a second, as the car rolled to a stop, she was willing to give up the whole project and retreat toward home as fast as possible.

"But it is just for a month here," she reminded herself. "Just four weeks. You have to go home after four weeks, to make room for the next class."

All the same, she felt small and solemn when she slid across the seat and out onto the gravel beside Mark. She tucked her hand under her mother's arm, edging closer than usual to her as they started walking over the soft grass of a lawn.

"Hey, there's Mr. Lister on the porch," Mark said.

"The man that interviewed you, Cathy, remember? Hi, Mr. Lister!"

"Hi, there," came the answer in a hearty voice. Footsteps hurried down a flight of wooden stairs, and Cathy's hand was seized in a broad, hairy one and emphatically pumped. "Hello, Cathy. Glad to have you here. Hello, Mrs. Wheeler, Mr. Wheeler. I'd like to have you meet Bob Zimmerman, the trainer who will have Cathy in charge."

Another hand grasped Cathy's, this one narrow and hard, and a voice much younger than she had expected said, "How do you do? I hope you brought a good supply of comfortable walking shoes, because you are going to hike a hundred miles during these next four weeks."

Mark gasped and crowded around in front of his sister. He was hardly able to contain himself until the rest of the introductions were acknowledged. "Hey, where's the dog?" he broke in when his chance came. "Can we see him now, or do we have to wait for you to give him to her?"

Mr. Zimmerman laughed. "I'm afraid you'll have to wait longer than that. We won't assign the dogs to the students for a couple of days. You see, at this point, the dogs are much more trained than the students, and the students have some catching up to do, so that it won't be embarrassing when they meet."

Mark fell silent, a sign that the information was a blow to his spirits. It was to Cathy's, too, and her feet wanted to drag on the steps to the porch when Mr. Lister took her arm to show her into the house and to where her room was located on the ground floor.

It was a good room, not at all the Burton-type barrack Cathy had so disliked. There was a big double bed, a table and chair, a dresser, a roomy cupboard and a large closet. A linoleum rug covered the floor, giving it a cool, summer cottage effect, and there were three wide windows open to the summer breeze. Another door on the closet side of the room led into a bathroom, which she would have to share with the student in the next room, but, compared to Burton, sharing with one person was real privacy, and the bedroom itself was to be hers alone. Mark and her father brought in her suitcases from the car, and, by the time her dresses were hung in the closet, her shoes arranged neatly on the floor, and her portable typewriter—a gift from her parents for her fifteenth birthday, two weeks ago—set on the table, some of the strangeness was yielding to an atmosphere of hominess.

"There," her father said, stowing her suitcases in the back of the closet, "that takes care of about everything, doesn't it? Anything else you can think of?"

"No, this is fine, thank you," Cathy replied, fingering the chair at the table. "Probably I won't even need this much stuff. It's only going to be four weeks."

But perhaps her smile was a trifle wan, for her mother said, a bit too brightly, "You'll be as comfortable here as at home. I wouldn't mind staying here myself. Now I suppose we'd better start back, if there's nothing more for us to do. Mr. Lister says it's a rule that the families must be gone before suppertime, and it's close to five now."

Mark tapped the lid of the typewriter case. "You'll write us a letter as soon as you get your dog, won't you? We ought to know what its name is and what kind it is, so we'll know what to call it when you come home."

"I surely will," Cathy promised, and went with her

family into the sitting room, which was right outside her door.

Soon they were gone. She heard the sound of their feet on the porch steps, the triple slam of the car doors and the crunch of the wheels on the gravel. Then she was alone, sitting in a lumpy, over-stuffed chair, listening to the sounds of other families talking in other rooms to other students.

But, in spite of her loneliness, excitement was beginning to fizz in her again, like carbonated water. This school was going to be very different from Burton. She could feel it.

One proof came in the form of supper, when the last of the departing friends and relatives had called good-by from the porch and the general confusion had faded to the comparative quiet of occasional drawers being shut, a wire clothes hanger or two being dropped on the floor and, outside, the stir of wind in the tree tops. Mr. Zimmerman appeared from nowhere, to call everyone into the sitting room and direct them from there to the dining room around the corner. Table places were quickly assigned, and Cathy found herself sniffing the spicy steam of spaghetti and meat balls. Remembering the meals at Burton, she was cautious about the first taste, but only the first. Nothing but her shyness amid these new surroundings prompted her to refuse a second helping when it was offered.

Another proof was the group of people who were gathered at the table. There were five of them besides herself and Mr. Zimmerman, and they were as different from the people she knew at Burton as though they had been born on a different planet. There was Mrs. Hanley, who introduced herself as a housewife and the mother of three children.

133

"Now that the three are in school all day," she said, "I can have some time for myself, to shop or visit or do what I please during those hours. That's why I want a dog. Maybe he'll help me work off the effects of being too fond of my own cooking, too."

The girl who had the room next to Cathy's was Miss Jardin. She was twenty-two, and studying music in the graduate school of the state university. Her reason for wanting a dog, she said, was that she had walked head on into just one too many doors with her cane last year.

There was Mr. Ingalls, a lawyer who had lost his sight in a car accident during the past winter and was anxious to avoid the sorry impression he would make in the courtroom by entering it clinging dependently to the arm of his client or an assistant. There was Mr. Gordon, a young radio technician, who had a chuckle that infected everyone, and who explained that he wanted a dog so he could make his calls by bus, because he didn't trust his wife's driving. And there was Dr. Bradson, who reminded Cathy somewhat of her father, and who, to her amazement, turned out to be a chemistry professor in a university.

"My reason for being here," he said a little sadly, "is that my poor old Fritz wore out from glaring at restless students for ten years. He went to sleep one night and never woke up. They say I've come for a replacement for him, but it's really for a successor, because, as Thomas Jefferson said of Benjamin Franklin in Paris, Fritz can only be succeeded, not replaced."

Cathy was more impressed than she could put into words. Nobody acted as if any of these achievements were wonderfully remarkable. They seemed to take it for granted that, because a person was unable to see, it didn't mean he was automatically incapable of accomplishing anything greater than caning chair bottoms or tying brooms for the remainder of his life. She pretended to be as casual as they were about it, but a secret elation began bubbling inside her.

She and the rest had one thing in common, however. That was a grand impatience to receive the dogs that were to be theirs. As though the return to the sitting room after supper were a pre-arranged signal, questions on how soon the dogs would arrive and why they wouldn't come sooner were peppering Mr. Zimmerman from every side, even before everyone had located a comfortable seat.

"It all depends on how you work out with Juno," Mr. Zimmerman said from the near end of the room. "You have plenty to learn from her first. If you do pretty well, maybe you'll get your own dogs Tuesday, but I'm making no promises. Except for Dr. Bradson. He'll get his dog tomorrow, because he doesn't need to try out with Juno."

"Thanks be to Providence for that." A cigarette lighter clicked, and Dr. Bradson exhaled slowly. "Juno and I conceived an instant dislike for each other upon our original meeting, and I am sure out tastes haven't changed during the years. Why don't you tell them who Juno is?"

"Juno is an old dog who never makes mistakes," Mr. Zimmerman said, and both men laughed. "She's smarter than any student I've had yet, so don't think you'll outwit her tomorrow and get away with what you think are shortcuts."

This was as much as he would say about Juno that evening, although he went on for an hour or more, talking of the advantages of having a guide dog and the responsibilities that were also a part of owning one. "People will be judging you by the appearance of your dog, by his grooming, his health and his general attitude—whether he looks contented or spiritless or vicious—and in a way, they'll be right, because your dog is as dependent on you for a good life as you are on him. And he is just as entitled to it. What's more, you should have perfect control over your dog at all times, because every guide dog is judged by the behavior of yours, and a few idiots who are too stupid or too cute to master their animals can do a fair job of ruining things for those who do. The best-trained dog on earth isn't much more useful than a pet turtle if all the doors in town are shut against him."

Cathy's head was so full of new ideas and food for thought by the end of Mr. Zimmerman's lecture that she was certain she would not sleep enough that night to pay for getting into bed, but it seemed as though she had no more than pulled the sheet over herself before the clock on the wall outside her door was chiming six. Immediately afterward, it chanted six rapid cuckoos, to show there had been no miscounting. She sighed drowsily and hoped you were supposed to add the chimes and the cuckoos together to mean twelve, but five minutes later, she heard Mr. Zimmerman knocking on each of the bedroom doors and announcing loudly that breakfast would be ready in half an hour.

It was the start of a busy day. There was an hour after breakfast for straightening up the rooms and doing what other odd tasks might be left. Then Mr. Zimmerman called the class into the sitting room and introduced them to Juno moving from student to student to let them examine her.

"Why, it's nothing but an empty harness!" Mrs. Hanley objected. "Where's this marvelous dog you were dangling in front of us?"

Dr. Bradson chuckled. "That marvelous dog is Mr. Zimmerman. There is something about these dog trainers that causes them to have a split personality, and they always imagine the second half as being four-footed and named Juno."

"Juno's as real a beast as you can handle today," Mr. Zimmerman said calmly, in answer to the groans that escaped Mr. Gordon and Miss Jardin. He passed the harness to Cathy, holding to the chest strap while she felt of the steel frame of the handle and its padded leather hand grip. "Juno responds to four main commands: forward, left, right and halt. She will lead you to any destination you want, provided you know enough about getting there to give her the proper directions at the proper times. If she stops without a command from you, it's a sign that you are at the top of a step or a curb, or at the bottom of one, or that there is an obstruction in your path. It's up to you to slide your foot ahead, to find out what's there, and to tell her what to do next. Any questions?" He paused, but no one spoke. "Fine! If you have no problems, I should have none. Since you're the youngest, Cathy, let's have you test fly her first."

Cathy stood up, confident that this empty-harness foolishness could not be more simple. Remembering what she had learned in the lecture last night, she grasped the handle in her left hand and waited. She knew Mr. Zimmerman was still holding the other end, for the leather braces stayed taut and level midway up her thigh, but nothing happened.

A full minute went by before Mr. Zimmerman said

quietly, "Your dog won't move unless you give him the command."

"Oh! Go! I mean, forward," she said hastily and giggled, not because it was funny but because she was embarrassed. She was grateful to the rest of the class for not laughing. They were paying strict and sober attention she could tell by their silence, but perhaps it was sympathetic as well, for their chance at mistakes was coming, too.

"Use your dog's name at the beginning of a command," Mr. Zimmerman reminded her, "so you are sure you have his attention."

"Juno, forward," Cathy repeated.

There was a firm tug on the harness. She followed, and it led her across the room to the door of the porch.

"Open the door," Mr. Zimmerman said, "and tell your dog where you want to go from there. The rest of you," he added over his shoulder to the class, "link arms and walk along behind us. This is your golden opportunity to profit by example."

Cathy obeyed, ordering Juno forward onto the porch . . . and then left toward the steps. She wasn't quite certain of where the steps were, though, and she began to drag back on the harness in an effort to slow it down. At the same time, she lengthened her stride, shuffling her feet far past one another as advance scouts to detect the sudden drop she expected.

"Oh, no," Mr. Zimmerman said. "I told you your dog would warn you of a step by halting at the edge of it. If you don't trust your dog, there's no sense in using him. You'll make him untrustworthy yourself by hesitating when you think there's something to be watched out for, because he'll recognize you aren't putting much faith in him, and he'll get sloppy about telling you what you obviously don't believe. Give Juno a double right turn, and we'll try this stair approach from the door again."

They had to try it twice more before Cathy's performance was acceptable. She could see the logic of Mr. Zimmerman's reasons, nor did she doubt that his Juno had the best of intentions, but absolute trust in a strange trainer or an unknown dog didn't happen all in a minute when toe bruising, tooth jarring experience had taught her that even her own parents forgot to mention the presence of curbs or stairs. As for Mark, she had yet to walk more than a block with him without once hearing him say, "Oops, there was a curb there!" as she gasped for the breath that had been jolted from her.

The practicing with Juno continued throughout the morning and the afternoon. Everyone had several turns at the stairs, the drive and the sidewalk, while those who were temporarily spectators trailed along in the rear, guided by Mr. Zimmerman's voice and doing their utmost to remember what not to do when Juno was theirs again. They spent the evening discussing their adventures and asking questions, and Mr. Zimmerman gave them a lesson in correcting Juno, in case she should make a mistake.

"If human beings aren't perfect, you can't insist that a dog must be, regardless of how well trained he is. He forgets or gets distracted or has a lazy day, just the same as people, and they have nothing against doing things the easy way, if they figure there's no penalty involved. Unless you correct a piece of carelessness immediately and definitely, you may very well be smashing your face against a post some day or vanishing from sight down an open manhole or saying your farewell to the world from under the wheels of a truck."

Cathy listened closely to Mr. Zimmerman's directions on the most effective manner of holding the leash in order to restore Juno's attention to her work by a single jerk. When he brought Juno's empty harness and choke collar to her for a demonstration, she was quite ready. Juno had been so unswervingly right in everything today, and she had done so many things wrong, that it was a real pleasure this evening to snap the leash taut and bark, "Juno, phooey!"

Tuesday was a repetition of Monday, except that the routine was more familiar, and the day passed more swiftly. Mr. Zimmerman was vague about when the flesh-and-blood Junos would be theirs, however, and by the middle of Wednesday morning, a fear was growing in Cathy that perhaps he wouldn't ever consider five of them worthy of handling a live dog. Dr. Bradson received his dog on Monday, of course, a big, silent German Shepherd named Wolf, and was going in to town twice a day with Mr. Zimmerman, for training on the downtown streets, which made the delay of the other dogs that much more tantalizing.

Cathy was thinking of this at the noon dinner, stabbing her fork into the last fragment of her slice of lemon pie and pretending that, like Dr. Bradson, she had a dog lying on her feet under the table, when Mr. Zimmerman cleared his throat with exaggerated thoroughness. In the abrupt hush that followed, he said casually, "You won't be enjoying the sunshine for a while this afternoon, I'm afraid. You'll be staying in your rooms for an hour or so, starting now." He allowed this to sink in before adding, the tone of a grin deepening his voice, "I talked to the kennel this morning. Your monsters will be here in about half an hour."

There was a cheer from all sides of the table, a burst of conversation and then a scramble for the rooms.

Cathy stationed herself on the edge of her bed nearest the windows, to hear the car the instant it rolled into the driveway. The clock in the sitting room chimed the quarter hour, but after that, its ticking slowed until it sounded as if there were a space of five minutes between each swing of the pendulum. Just when she thought she could stand the waiting no longer, a motor hummed into the driveway at last. Her heart jumped so high that she almost missed the knock on her door that came at the same time.

It was Mr. Zimmerman. "I'm passing out ice breakers," he explained, pushing a pan into her hand. "Take a fistful of this, and your popularity is assured. It's better than Chanel No. 5."

Cathy dug in willingly. It was a mixture of ground meat and meal of some sort, not much more appetizing to smell than it was delightful to feel, but at this point it would have had to be a genuine stench and downright slime for her to notice. She sat tense and stiff, listening to the trainer tap on the other doors in turn, peddling his ice breakers.

Suddenly a stillness was everywhere, as though the house were holding its breath. It was broken by a scrabble of toenails on the floor of the porch and a sharp, "Phooey!" from Mr. Zimmerman. The screen door banged. Paws padded across the sitting room, and Mr. Zimmerman said at her door, "Here she is, Cathy. She's a year-old German Shepherd. Her name is Trudy, and she's all yours."

There was the snick of the leash being unhooked, and the click of the door being shut. Then nothing.

Cathy sat rigid, not daring to flutter an eyelash. What if Trudy took a dislike to her? What if she didn't want to belong to anybody? What if she were afraid in these new surroundings?

The questions were answered by a cold, wet nose poking into her hand. Cathy uncrooked her fingers, and the food disappeared, not snatched but not nibbled warily either. A tongue like a warm, wet strip of kid cleaned her palm and between her fingers, and she realized that the breeze fanning the lock of hair on her forehead was being whipped up by the wagging of a tail.

"Trudy," she said, touching the head that was as broad between the ears as her hand. They were big ears, too, cupped at the base and tapering at the tips like the petals of a tulip, and the short, thick fur that covered them was as soft as kitten velvet. "Hi, Trudy! You are beautiful."

Trudy's jaw closed on her wrist, not biting it but locking it within a cage of large, strong teeth. Cathy knew a flash of mild alarm, but the tail was wagging faster than ever, and the gentle shake her wrist received was plainly not intended to hurt.

Her message not understood, Trudy released the wrist and, bobbing her head to Cathy's shoe, gave the laces a hopeful tug.

"You want to play?" Cathy asked, as thrilled as she was relieved. She slid from the bed onto her knees, both hands rubbing the coarse, sleek coat. "Trudy, you beauty!"

Her face was washed from cheek to chin in a double

sweep of an eager, wet tongue, and their friendship was permanently sealed from that moment.

But the hours that followed, and the days and the weeks, were far removed from a happy vacation of playtime. Each morning and each afternoon, the class was packed into the station wagon and driven to the heart of town, where, for two or three hours, they tramped singly or in pairs along the busy streets, crossing at noisy corners where there were traffic lights and at noisy corners where there were none, entering small shops and spacious department stores, climbing stairs and descending stairs, riding elevators, going through revolving doors, weaving their way among crowds of shoppers, or maneuvering the obstacle courses of toy-strewn suburban sidewalks, always with Mr. Zimmerman walking watchfully at their side or a few paces behind. In the evenings, they discussed the day's successes or mishaps, or practiced correcting techniques on Juno again, or Mr. Zimmerman read excerpts from books and articles on various aspects of owning a guide dog.

After exercising their dogs in the yard around eight-thirty or nine, the students were free to relax as they pleased, but ten o'clock never failed to find Cathy too weary for anything but tumbling into bed.

Not only was she worn out physically at the finish of a day, but often she was downright discouraged as well. There was so much to learn, and so much to remember. The art of walking itself, of keeping a natural and even balance while gripping an ever-pulling handle in her left hand, did not come to her overnight. More than once she performed a quick set of grace steps to straighten her leftward tilt, only to bring a pained yelp from Trudy, whose feet were seldom at the safe distance Cathy imagined them.

Furthermore, Trudy was not the irreproachable paragon of doggy virtues that Juno was. She had her training down pat and could distinguish right from left more unfalteringly than Cathy herself, but she had no qualms about ignoring a curb if the station wagon were just up the next block, or about halting where there was no curb if a patch of grass or a fire hydrant took her fancy. Also, she had a habit of looking backward, to check on Mr. Zimmerman's whereabouts. This trick drifted the pair off the sidewalk onto a lawn one day and sent Cathy sprawling over a tricycle another time.

"It's your own fault, Cathy," Mr. Zimmerman said, helping to disentangle her from the maze of wheels and handle bars. "You're not tough enough on her. Those little love taps you call corrections don't even make her blink. Really jerk her off her feet a couple of times, and she'll get the idea. She is a good dog, one of the best I've trained, but you're going to ruin her. Show her who's boss. I've seen you do it on Juno."

Cathy nodded meekly, but what she and Trudy both understood was that a world of difference lay between Trudy's sensitive nature and the smug, nonexistent Juno. A single sharp word wilted Trudy's perky ears flat to her head, and if an apology were not immediate, including sweet talk and caresses, the curl drooped from her tail, her hind quarters sagged, and the spark of love threatened to die out within her forever. Mr. Zimmerman claimed this was sheer dramatics, but, although he was wiser in the ways of dogs than anybody Cathy had ever met, an element of doubt locked her arm whenever she raised it to deliver a correction, and

Trudy went blithely on, unaware that she had been reprimanded.

"I might as well be going home, too," Cathy said disconsolately to Dr. Bradson as they crouched together, nearly shoulder to shoulder, on the porch, giving their dogs their daily grooming. It was Dr. Bradson's last afternoon at the training school, because, having had a dog already, he needed only a two-week get-acquainted course to weld himself and Wolf into a working team. "I've walked a hole in my shoe and a blister on my toe, and I'm still as bad at handling Trudy as I was the first day. I can't seem to do anything right."

"Maybe the trouble is that you're trying to do everything at once," Dr. Bradson said. "Why not concentrate on one thing or a couple for a while, keeping your balance, for instance, or remembering to praise Trudy for stopping at curbs properly. Let the other things ride for a day or so, until you can afford to put your full attention on them." The strokes of the wire brush he was using on Wolf swished in rhythm to his advice. "There's an old, Confucius-type proverb I like to think of when I get a class of freshmen at the university who seem to be about as chemistry-minded as Wolf here: 'Better to light a single candle than sit and curse the dark.' So I content myself with lighting the little candle of merely waking them up to an understanding of what chemistry is all about, instead of setting out on the impossible job of turning the lot of them into first-rate chemists. Sometimes it has happened that my one candle uncovers a few students I wouldn't have noticed otherwise, and I have some chemists anyhow."

Cathy pondered these suggestions and repeated the proverb to herself a score of times as she and Trudy and Mr. Zimmerman tramped away the third week of her training. A morning of concentrating on saying, "Good girl, Trudy," for each command Trudy performed perfectly actually wore the words into her memory almost to the depth of a habit by afternoon, and a day of concentrating on her posture and matching her stride to Trudy's so that their feet were never tangling together in the same place at the same instant brought praise from Mr. Zimmerman. Bit by bit, she began to conquer, or at least control, her other faults, too, but on the Monday of the final week, Mr. Zimmerman shattered her triumph by announcing:

"Today you solo. I've spent three weeks spoon feeding you. What you don't know now, you'll either learn today or never know. Everybody is on his own."

It was too soon! Cathy tightened her grip on Trudy's leash and burrowed her spine into the cushions of the station wagon seat, flooded by visions of the dozens of details she and Trudy were still shaky on. How could they risk a trip alone? If they had a few more days of practice, three or two or one . . .

But Mr. Zimmerman's decisions were law. There was no begging off. And of course, as luck would have it, she and Trudy were in the front seat of the station wagon today, which meant they were automatically elected to go first.

"We're parked about the middle of the block," Mr. Zimmerman said, holding Trudy for her while Cathy climbed out of the car. "Go up to the corner, turn right and go straight ahead for two blocks. Turn right again for another two blocks. Right at the next corner, two more blocks, another right and come back to the station wagon. Got it?"

She had it—just a great, uncomplicated square, two

blocks long on each side. It was also almost a mile of unsupervised walking, in which practically any disaster might be lurking to overtake her.

Cathy closed her fingers on the handle of Trudy's harness, delayed as much as she could in arranging the leash in her hand . . . and finally said, "Forward, Trudy."

Her lack of confidence must have traveled down the harness braces to the dog, for Trudy's response was a slow and meandering amble, not in the least like her usual brisk trot. They reached the corner, however, without serious difficulty, and made shambling but steady progress down the sidewalk that led them beyond the view of the station wagon.

"Come on, Trudy," Cathy said nervously. "Let's hurry." She judged they were approaching the end of the block, and she wasn't anxious to poke across even the quietest of streets at this speed.

Trudy's feet moved faster. In fact, she leaned into the harness and began to haul Cathy onward like a horse drawing a wagon. Cathy was forced to do a pair of skipping steps to catch up, and grass abruptly replaced the pavement under her shoes. A flurry of challenging barks from across the street told the reason.

Cathy dragged her guide onto the walk again, forgetting to say, "Trudy, phooey!" until Trudy was reluctantly inching forward toward the corner and looking back at the other dog in sulky defiance.

They halted at the curb. That is, Cathy stopped shoving the harness ahead, and Trudy stopped resisting the shove. The other dog ceased his barking, which Cathy thought was as grand a blessing as the momentary absence of traffic on the street.

"Trudy, forward," she commanded and gave the harness another push.

Sluggish but obedient, Trudy stepped into the street. It seemed to Cathy that they were proceeding somewhat at an angle from the spot where she would have supposed the opposite curb to be and she clutched the harness all the harder, thankful she did not have to depend on her own senses to steer her to safety. This was such a wide street, too, wider than any she had crossed with Mr. Zimmerman. The rough concrete beneath her feet went on and on and on.

"Trudy," she urged uneasily, "can't you hurry?"

At any minute, a car might round a corner and come roaring down on them. She extended her free hand to give the dog an encouraging pat, but Trudy plodded on, unaffected, her ears flat, her head hanging, the picture of sullen dejection. And still there was no rising curb.

A horrible possibility froze Cathy's pulse. As if to confirm it, a screen door slammed off to the right of them. They were not going to hit the other curb. Trudy had chosen to lead her in the street itself, rather than on the sidewalk where they belonged.

Panic seized Cathy, added to by the distant but growing rumble of a car approaching from the rear. "Trudy, phooey!" Her arm swept up and back, jerking the leash with all the power of desperation. Trudy uttered a stifled yip that savored more of astonishment than pain, and her limpness vanished. Swerving to the right, she gained the parallel curbing in the space of five steps. Three more carried her and Cathy across the grass terrace and onto the walk. They were well on their way up it toward the next corner by the time the car whizzed by on the street.

At the corner, Cathy's, "Trudy, right," produced a quarter turn as snappy and precise as could be done by a file of soldiers on parade. There were children playing on this block. Tricycle bells jingled, and metal wagons clunked hollowly, but Trudy wove in and out among them without slacking her pace or allowing so much as the hem of Cathy's skirt to brush an obstacle. Only once, when a puppy hurtled, yapping, against the screen of its front door, did she waver, and then a short, "Trudy!" from Cathy, steadied the wobble like magic.

They accomplished their second street crossing with the directness of an arrow. The dregs of Cathy's scare crumpled to dust and sifted off on the breeze. Her legs and Trudy's were moving in a smooth, effortless rhythm that had somehow come about by itself. Trudy's head was up, her ears perked, and not a trace of resentment was visible anywhere.

Exhilaration surged sparkling in Cathy. For the first time in over a year she was out on her own, alone, by herself, unescorted by any other human being, restricted to the guidance of no one's arm, the whim of no one's voice. She knew how a bird must feel on discovering the door of his cage is open. She was free again, independent and whole, and it was a thousand times more glorious than she had remembered.

When they halted at the curb before their third street crossing, Cathy couldn't resist bending to give Trudy a quick hug of appreciation. "Trudy, you're wonderful!"

Trudy's tail swayed briefly. Her nose lifted to touch Cathy's cheek, then switched back for a survey of the street ahead. She was all business, now that she was assured of what her business was. From alert head to tip-curled tail, her pose said, "This is just the beginning."

8

TRUDY BECAME the central fixture in the Wheeler household inside a week. Mark greeted her with open arms, exercising her in the yard, romping with her in the living room and talking to her confidentially as if she were his dearest playmate. Mr. Wheeler cut down a set of springs from an old twin bed and put castors on it so that it could be rolled like a trundle bed under Cathy's during the daytime. Mrs. Wheeler donated four feather pillows and a discarded quilt from the attic to make a suitable mattress. The whole family went on a shopping tour that was as much to select the right food and water dishes for Trudy as it was to buy school shoes for Cathy and Mark, and all of them, including Cathy, marveled at the ease with which Trudy piloted her around counters and among shoppers. And Cathy, reaching out a hand first thing in the morning or sometimes when she woke during the night to touch the furry bulk on the low bed beside hers, planned happily for the year at Wilson High that would begin on the Wednesday after Labor Day.

Then, on Tuesday afternoon, the doorbell rang, and there stood Joan Norton on the step.

"Hi, Cathy," she said, walking in as though nothing were more natural than her presence here. "Remember me? I saw you and your dog go past our house a while ago, and I got inspired to come over for a chat. It sure has been an age since our last one."

It was indeed, Cathy reflected, for, to her knowledge, they never had had a chat, although they had been classmates and not too distant neighbors since the fourth grade. Joan was one of the girls who had been at Pete Sheridan's birthday party last year, the party to which Cathy hadn't been invited, but, of course, Joan couldn't be blamed for that. The fact that Cathy hadn't ever thought of her as a friend didn't stem from any real dislike of Joan. It was just that the things that interested them were always poles apart, with nothing in between on which to build a friendship, and Cathy couldn't imagine what had actually brought her schoolmate here today.

Maybe Joan felt an explanation was due, too, for she said, as soon as they were seated together in the living room, "I hear you are starting in at Wilson tomorrow. Your little brother told me. He says you're going to hire some of the kids to do your reading for you. Do you have anybody yet?"

Cathy shook her head. "Not yet." She rubbed Trudy's flank, pressed against her knee as Trudy stretched her neck to investigate the smell of the newcomer's shoes. "We thought it would be better to wait until I can ask somebody in my classes, somebody who'll have the same homework to read anyway."

"But it doesn't have to be somebody in your classes, does it?" Joan asked quickly. "I mean it could be anybody who could manage the time and is qualified to do it? It might be we're in some of the same classes anyhow."

Cathy turned toward her in surprise. "Are you asking for the job?"

"Sure, if it's all right with you." Joan laughed and gave a nervous sort of wriggle that produced a stiff-petticoat sounding rustle. "I don't care how much it pays, or if it pays anything. I just feel it's the kind of thing a person ought to do for another if they can. I've been an A student for the past three years, so you don't have to worry about that, and I'm a good reader."

The edges of Cathy's smile pulled a little taut at the implication that she was the object of ennobling charity, but the offer was too attractive a solution to her biggest problem to be passed by for the sake of an over-sensitive pride. She accepted gratefully, and the two girls set to work at once on arranging the details, with the help of a couple of bottles of root beer from the refrigerator.

"Gee, listen to that!" Joan interrupted herself suddenly as the mantel clock struck five. "I'm supposed to be home eating supper. How will it be if I stop by tomorrow about eight, and we can go to school together? You are taking the bus, aren't you?"

"Sure," Cathy answered, rising to follow her guest to the door, "but you don't have to come way up here for me. Trudy and I will meet you at the bus stop, or else on the eight-ten bus."

"Trudy?" repeated Joan blankly. "Who's that? You don't mean the dog, do you? Are you bringing him to school?"

An element of disapproving incredulity in her tone nettled Cathy. "*She* is bringing me," she said, emphasizing the pronoun. "That is what *she* is here for."

Joan, who had the screen door partly open, let it click shut and stepped into the house again. "What's he going to do during class? Won't that make you awfully conspicuous? I mean, everybody in the neighborhood runs to the windows to watch you and him go by when you're only walking on the street. Imagine the commotion you'd cause in school!"

Put like that, Cathy could imagine the scene, although it was a possibility that had not occurred to her before. "But I have permission from the principal—"

"Well, it's up to you," Joan said, still disapproving. "I'll call for you tomorrow anyhow, in case you change your mind. It's only that I thought it might be better if the kids got used to you first, the fact that you're—well, you know—different. Later on, maybe, if you wanted to bring the dog, it wouldn't be such a shock."

That was the shot that did it. "I'll see," Cathy hedged, but the outcome of her "seeing" was almost a foregone certainty. The weak point of her armor was that word *different*, and the scars beneath it were not healed enough to withstand the impact of a direct hit.

"I think you are being very foolish," was her mother's comment when she broached the matter to her family that evening. "You're making a big mistake, and you're going to regret it," her father declared.

Mark said, "You're plain nuts. Why do you want to be so goofy?"

But none of them had to lie awake that night, battling the troop of spear-tipped memories that attacked Cathy without mercy: of Pete in the alley, unaccountably strange and ill at ease; of a birthday party three houses away, in which she could not share, only stand and listen; of Emma mumbling, "I wouldn't go to public school. They're mean to blind kids"; of Ida exclaiming, "I'd die of shame!"; of Miss Creel snapping, "You'll be singled out and watched in everything you do as if you were a freak. Half of your classmates will snicker behind your back because you are different, and the other half will embarrass you by feeling sorry for you."

By morning, the battle was lost. Shortly after eight o'clock, Cathy hurriedly shut the front door between herself and the wildly whining Trudy and departed for the bus stop, her arm linked through Joan Norton's.

Joan was in high spirits. "We're going to get there early, I think. That means I'll have time to show you around a little. You haven't ever been inside the high school, have you?"

"No," Cathy admitted. "I've seen it from the outside often enough, but I haven't any idea where the rooms are located."

"Well, don't worry about trying to remember it all at once," Joan said, giving Cathy's arm a reassuring squeeze with her elbow. "I'll copy your schedule for myself this morning and meet you after every class, so you won't have to ask anybody else to take you to the next one. Just wait for me. I like this good deed business."

Again Cathy's pride winced, but she was hardly in a position to protest aloud, and Joan proved to be as good as her word. Better even, for throughout the day she was as prompt as the bell in appearing to whisk Cathy from this class to that with minutes to spare, and not once did she forget to warn in advance of a step or a raised, toe-snagging threshold. If she had any flaws as a guide, perhaps it was her tendency to be louder and more distinct than was quite necessary when she said, "The stairs begin right here," or, "This is the bottom step. Don't trip."

But that was a tiny annoyance to take note of in the whirlwind confusion that buffeted Cathy from the assembly bell in the morning to the dismissal bell in the afternoon. Teachers and students were posted in the halls, to direct traffic, to prevent running or pushing and to keep talking to a minimum between classes, but to her ears, conditioned by the lax atmosphere and relatively small number of pupils at Burton, the surge of two thousand students in a rush to get from one class to another in the five-minute passing time was nothing short of pandemonium. The stamp of feet mounting the stairs, the shuffle of feet descending the stairs, and the tap and patter and scuffle of feet on the tile floors merged in a single dull roar like surf. She was aware that some of those feet must belong to people she used to know in grade school, but she had always been too busy with Pete to form any other real friendships, and now her year of isolation had made them all into strangers, and made her a stranger to them, so that she was lost in an uncharted sea of noise.

Her sense of direction was drowned utterly. Even her sense of balance was shaken. She felt dizzy, and clung to Joan's arm the tighter. Not until she felt the panting sigh that escaped from her lungs when she gained the quiet and order of each classroom did she realize that she must have been holding her breath the length of the halls. It went against her grain to agree with anything Miss Creel said, but it was true that this was not how she remembered public school. But that was because her other observations had been through her eyes instead of her ears, and it did not mean, she told herself grimly, that her career at Wilson High was doomed to failure. Only, what would have become of Trudy in all this turmoil?

She missed Trudy often during that day, wondered how she was getting on at home without her, tried to imagine how it would be to have her lying beside her desk and revolved again and again the reasons for not bringing her to school. But it was in English, her last class of the afternoon, that she first was sure that it was good to have left Trudy at home.

"306," Joan said, reading the schedule before they started off to find the room. "That's Miss Vincent. Oh, you poor kid! How did you ever let them give you her for English?"

"Why? What's she like?" Cathy hugged her armload of notebooks and folders closer to her, picturing Miss Creel.

"She is *the* worst luck you could have," Joan said positively. "She is purely diabolical. Nobody hands out more homework or flunks more kids than she does. There's practically no pleasing her. Of course," she added on a virtuous note that a private corner of Cathy's mind warned was something that must be frequently forgiven, if she and Joan were to stay friends, "I had no trouble in her class. We got along fine, but I was the only one, and I had to work at it."

Miss Vincent's version of herself, delivered without preliminaries as soon as the class had settled in their seats, was slanted from a different point of view, but she spat out the words as though she were biting heads off tacks, and, in Cathy's judgment, they amounted to the same information as Joan's:

"All right, class. I know there is a rumor circulating in this school that I don't like children. That is not true. I am very fond of children. However, a classroom is a place of orderliness and discipline where you come to learn, not to play baby games. I will not tolerate fidgeting, inattention, or slovenly work from my pupils. If you are willing to accept these conditions, we will have a happy, profitable year together. If you aren't, you may as well get up and get out now."

She paused, as if she expected someone really would get up and leave. Cathy's skin prickled with the effort of willing herself inconspicuous. Her mental picture of Miss Vincent was so vivid she could almost have painted it: metallic blue eyes behind steel-rimmed spectacles perched on the ridge of a high, sharp nose, gray-white hair puffed on top of her head, thin mouth, back stiff and shoulders square as those of a major of the women's marines. Such a hush chilled the room that the crackle of a tiny scrap of paper, probably no bigger than a gum wrapper, was audible from wall to wall.

"Young lady!" snapped Miss Vincent. "You are fidgeting. Stop it immediately."

The crackling stopped, punctuated by a faint gasp, quickly choked off, too.

Miss Vincent stepped nearer the front row of desks. "I have here a set of paper slips on which I have marked the number of each seat in this room. When you receive the one bearing your seat number, write your name on it. If you can't see the board from where you are now, or if you have difficulty hearing from the rear of the room, or if you have any other physical disability or problem I should take into account in making my permanent seating arrangement, write that down, too."

Cathy, in the front seat of the row closest the door, was the first to receive her slip. She heard it flip onto her desk, and dropped her hand on it to keep it from blowing away in the breeze of Miss Vincent's passing by, but she waited until she was sure Miss Vincent was too busy doling out the other slips to pounce on fidgeters before she dared fumble in her purse for the pencil she had brought for just such an emergency. Using her left thumb and forefinger as line guides, she carefully wrote her name between them, wishing she'd practiced her penmanship more seriously when she could see. Then, underneath, she wrote, "I am blind."

A slow heat climbed into her cheeks and spread across her forehead as she reached over her shoulder for the papers being passed forward from the rear and added her note to the pile. Her month at the training school, listening to the talk and jokes of Dr. Bradson, Mrs. Hadley, Mr. Gordon and the rest had robbed that word "blind" of its sting for her. They all said it so casually, never going out of their way to avoid it nor faltering on it as if it were of any more significance in a sentence than "peanut butter" or "television," that her attitude had changed from shock to wonder and gradually to an acceptance almost as casual as theirs. She could say it or hear it or write it now without a quiver most of the time, but a lot depended on whether the reactions of the other person were also matter of fact, and she had disquieting doubts about that being Miss Vincent's reaction to anything.

The suspense did not last long. Miss Vincent rapidly collected the slips from the front desks and walked to her own desk. Her chair rolled a little on squeaky casters, and again silence was thick in the room, except for the brisk shuffle of the papers as she checked through them.

Cathy stared down at her desk top, her shoulders mentally hunched to withstand any blow, but she jumped in spite of herself when the papers were suddenly slapped flat on the teacher's desk and the chair was pushed noisily back.

"Very well," Miss Vincent said, "I'll assign you your permanent seats tomorrow. Let it be understood from the start that there will be no favoritism in this class, no special consideration for anyone. You will pass or fail strictly on your merits as a student, and on nothing else. There will be no privileged persons in this group."

If she had been singled out by name, the fire in Cathy's face could hardly have burned hotter. She yearned to shrink to pencil size and lose herself from view inside the desk. It could only have been worse if Trudy were here, too, lying large and special and privileged in the aisle beside her feet.

Yet, there was a challenge in Miss Vincent's tartness. It would have been easy to hate her. Cathy wasn't sure she didn't already, but, at the same time, she was oddly excited, too. Here was her chance to prove to the Miss Creels and Miss Vincents, and even to herself, that she could make the grade on nothing but her own merits as well as anybody else. She *would* prove it, she vowed, clamping a sheet of paper into her Braille slate and poising her stylus about it, ready to note down every word that Miss Vincent would speak. She would prove it if she had to sit up studying all night each night until the end of the semester, to do it.

But Trudy was a different matter—poor Trudy, who came bounding shoulder-high to meet her mistress as Cathy and Joan turned onto the Wheelers' front walk late that afternoon. Cathy flung her books on the grass and went on her knees to hug her dog as tightly as it was possible to hug seventy pounds of wriggling bone and muscle.

"I hope you realize that you broke her heart, leaving her like that today," Mrs. Wheeler said from the doorway. "She whined and cried for hours after you'd gone, and spent the rest of the time pacing from window to window, looking for you to come home. Either you take her tomorrow, or you find a nice sanitarium for me to move to. This is more than I can stand."

"Oh, I can't," Cathy said, and dodged the tongue that was seeking to wipe her whole face. "Not tomorrow."

"Why not?" her mother asked. "What's to prevent it? You can't leave her home forever, or there's no sense in having her. You might better have bought yourself a pet kitten, and left the dog for someone who needed her."

"I do need her," Cathy said, and caught Trudy in another hug to assure herself that no one was going to break up their partnership. "But I can't take her to school just now. I can't!" Neither could she tell the reason why, not there on the front lawn, with Joan an interested audience. Perhaps not ever anyway.

"I think she's quite right, Mrs. Wheeler," Joan said earnestly. "You have no idea how crowded the high schools are these days. Trudy would be more of a nuisance than she is worth, especially when I'm so handy to take Cathy around. And I love doing it." Her laugh was half apologetic, half pleased. "It makes me feel important. You should have seen how the kids were looking at us today. Mostly it was because they were curious about Cathy, of course, but they noticed me, too."

Cathy released Trudy and gathered her books together. Her lips were a little stiff, but she said smoothly enough, "I'll see you tomorrow, Joan. Thanks a lot."

In her heart, as she entered the house and mounted

the stairs to put her things in her room, she was also thanking her mother for not commenting. If Joan was rather thoughtless about what she was likely to say, she had plenty of good points to offset it. There weren't many mere acquaintances who would so willingly volunteer for the duties of substitute guide dog, plus a double load of homework, for, as it turned out, she and Cathy were in none of the same classes. Joan was a full-fledged sophomore, while Cathy, having lost half a year of regular credits during her courses in typing and Braille, was still a second semester freshman.

"But that's fine with me," Joan insisted. "We have three study periods together, besides lunch hour. That's as much as we'd ever need to get your reading done, and I can easily do mine at home. I never go anywhere after school anyhow."

Reminding herself of this from time to time, Cathy managed to ease through Thursday and Friday of that week without too much pain. There were a few bad moments, such as Joan's invariable, "To the right more, forward a bit, now down," in a tone that must penetrate to every ear on the bus whenever Cathy dropped her fare in the box, or the equally high-pitched remark, "I guess they didn't ever expect to have blind students in that school or they wouldn't have used combination locks," when she spun the dial on Cathy's locker. But Joan was a good reader, rapid and distinct, there was no denying that and, between the reading at school and the things like algebra and Spanish vocabulary Cathy worked on by herself in the evenings, there were few idle minutes for brooding over minor stings.

To make up somewhat for her neglect of Trudy, she harnessed her the first thing Saturday morning and they set off on a long, carefree walk to nowhere in particular.

Trudy was not in a forgiving mood, however. She showed her feeling about the dullness of the past three days by lunging into her harness with all her strength and fairly dragging Cathy down the street at a speed that left her breathless, by stepping lightheartedly from curbs without a hint of warning, by craning her neck to stare interestedly in every direction but where she was headed, and by wilting ears, head and tail in blank bewilderment in response to "left" or "right," as though they were commands a thousandfold too foreign and complicated for her ever to comprehend. Several corrections with the leash, a quantity of scoldings and two retracings of part of the route until she consented to halt at the curbs properly finally straightened out the kinks, but, by then, the fun was gone from the walk, and both she and Cathy were tired of the whole idea.

"I guess I'll have to walk her daily after school," Cathy admitted to the family at lunch. "I didn't dream she could get so rusty in just a couple of days."

It wasn't rustiness, though. She understood that as well as Trudy did. The problem was plain boredom, spiced by a touch of disgruntlement at being reduced from a vital companion to a stay-at-home pet. Trudy was specially chosen and specially trained for a special job. She loved doing it, she wanted to do it, and there was no genuine reason why she couldn't do it—except when Cathy thought of Miss Vincent and of the things Joan said and, more than that, of the spectacle she would create appearing all at once with a dog when she had started without one.

It was a slippery rut Cathy had let Joan push her into that first day, and each day that she went farther along in it, the sides seemed to grow steeper and more unclimbable. Monday came and went . . . and Tuesday

. . . and Wednesday and the "maybe tomorrow" that she promised herself wistfully every night during her walk with Trudy was still "maybe tomorrow," when she woke in the morning. Perhaps if her classmates had been a little more friendly—but nearly the entire week passed by without anyone but Joan bothering to speak more than a scattered handful of words to her.

The one exception happened Friday noon, as Cathy was sitting in the cafeteria, waiting for Joan, who was buying milk for them at the counter. She assumed it was Joan who had returned when someone sat down beside her, but the dainty fragrance of cologne was not Joan's.

"Hello," the girl said, in a voice that was not quite unfamiliar. "Your name's Cathy Wheeler, isn't it? I'm Mary Beth Robertson. I'm in your English class."

Cathy turned toward her, as pleased as though she were Robinson Crusoe just discovering a human footprint on a desert island. "I've heard you answering questions in class."

"Oh, don't remind me!" Mary Beth's shudder bumped her shoulder against Cathy's, but her giggle belied any real dismay. "When Miss Vincent fixes those stony eyes on me, I practically froth at the mouth, I'm so scared. I always have an uncomfortable feeling in her class that I haven't done the right assignment. That's what I wanted to ask you about. We weren't supposed to prepare all twenty of those grammar exercises for today, were we?"

"I thought we were. Anyway, I did them all." Cathy reached for the paper folder under her unopened lunch. "The assignment might be in here, but this is probably the wrong folder."

"I'll take your word for it. I've heard you answering

in class, too, and if you did twenty, Mary Beth had better do twenty. I'll have to hustle, though. Thanks." Mary Beth stood up. "By the way, I saw you and your dog go by my house a couple of afternoons ago—Tuesday afternoon, I guess it was. He's gorgeous. I've been meaning to tell you, but there's no chance in Miss Vincent's class, and wherever else I see you, you're either rushing off to somewhere with your friend or she's busy talking to you in such a serious-looking way that I don't want to interrupt."

Cathy laughed. "I'm never in such a rush or too serious to be interrupted by somebody who wants to admire my dog. I think she's gorgeous, too."

"She!" Mary Beth echoed. "I beg your pardon—and hers. But if you don't mind my asking, how come you don't bring her to school?"

"I've been thinking about it," Cathy said slowly. She plucked at the rubber band around her lunch bag, hoping she didn't sound over eager. "She's perfectly trained and everything, but I've been sort of doubtful— There's such a crowd of kids here at Wilson."

"They wouldn't bother her, would they? Everybody ought to have sense enough to leave a dog like that alone. If you got permission to go on the PA system some morning and explain about her, that would take care of even the dumbest ones, wouldn't it?" Mary Beth sighed. "I know I'd love to have her in a class of mine, especially Miss Vincent's. I'd feel a good deal safer." She stopped. "Oh, here comes your friend. I'll see you in English."

Cathy nodded, smiling after her until the seat beside her was again filled, and a waxy carton of milk was pushed against her hand.

"Looks like I scared off your little visitor," Joan said,

obviously unregretful. "What did she want? To marvel at how brave you are to be going to high school when you're a poor blind child, like those women I was talking to on the bus yesterday?"

"No," Cathy said shortly. She poked her straw into the milk and unwrapped a sandwich. Joan was developing a talent not only for discovering people who did such marveling, but for repeating their well-meant condescensions frequently and with gusto. The women yesterday were the third marvelers this week. It was heartening for the spirit to be able to add carelessly, "Mary Beth just wanted to know something about today's homework."

"Wonder why she didn't ask me," Joan said above the rattle of her lunch bag as she fished in it for whatever she intended to eat first. "I know as much about your assignments as you do. And everybody's heard that I'm doing all your reading."

"That," Cathy said, biting into a slice of dill pickle, "I believe."

She halfway expected Joan to be angered by this and halfway wished she would be. For no definite reason she could name, she was in an ungenerous mood that prodded her to be irritated at Joan for the very things for which she ought to be constantly thanking her. Maybe it was the fault of the weather, spatting rain against the windows off and on the whole day and weighting the air indoors and out with a clammy sluggishness, or maybe it was nothing more than a Friday kind of restlessness. At any rate, although she did not exactly want the reproach of having started it, Cathy was in no humor to back away from a quarrel if one should offer.

It was Miss Vincent who obligingly put the spark to

the fuse. "Catherine, wait a minute, please," she said as the class was filing out at the end of the English period. "I want to speak to you."

Cathy sank into her seat, a shiver of foreboding crawling up her skin. She nodded mutely toward Miss Vincent's desk in response to the "Hi," that announced Joan was at hand, ready to take her to her locker.

"Now, then, Catherine," Miss Vincent said, coming over to them when the last of the class was gone, "I have a memo here from the principal's office concerning your student readers. Have you found someone in this class yet who can do the English work with you?"

"She doesn't have to," Joan said quickly. "I'm doing her reading for her. All of it. I volunteered."

"All of it?" Miss Vincent sounded far from being as impressed as Joan's smug statement invited her to be. "What about your own work? You are a sophomore, aren't you?"

"Yes, but I consider this good review work for me," Joan said in her virtuous voice. "I love to study, and I'm sure my work isn't suffering. Besides, I would gladly drop from an A to a B in a class or two if I had to, because I feel it's in a worth-while cause."

"Well, that is not how I feel about it," Miss Vincent said tartly. "It's sheer foolishness on your part to attempt it, and presumption on the part of anyone else to expect it of you. I suppose you are taking a full schedule, Catherine?"

"Yes, I am." Cathy's relief at finding it was not the results of her studying but merely the methods which were being criticized loosened her tongue. "I think Joan is working harder than she should, too. Perhaps, Miss Vincent, if you could suggest somebody in this class who might not mind reading English—"

166

"There are four or five girls I imagine might be interested. I'll speak to them about it Monday, if you like, and you can choose which you would prefer. I certainly think it would be a healthier arrangement for everyone than what you have now."

There was nothing in Miss Vincent's tone that encouraged smiling, but Cathy flashed her a swift one anyway. At this moment she almost liked her. "Thank you, Miss Vincent. I do appreciate this."

She had an idea that Joan was rather less enthusiastic, but how much less she did not learn until they were well beyond earshot of Miss Vincent's room, hurrying down the rainy front steps of the school on their way to catch the bus for home.

"That old crone!" Joan exploded finally, as if the steps were jarring fury from her. "Because she's a left-over from Noah's ark, she thinks she has a right to poke her nose into everybody's business. What does it matter to her who does what, as long as it gets done?"

Cathy jerked off her plastic kerchief. The rain had stopped temporarily, and having her ears covered up dimmed the vividness of her surroundings for her as effectively as wearing dark glasses used to do. "She had a note from the office, telling her to check."

"Only to check on whether you had readers or not. I'll bet it didn't say a word about switching a perfectly good arrangement around to suit herself. What's so unhealthy about me, I'd like to know? She acts like everybody is a juvenile delinquent on probation."

To Cathy's surprise, the arm linked through hers was actually shaking with indignation. Joan plunged ahead through the depths of puddles and into the midst of slippery drifts of leaves without paying the slightest attention to wet feet or splashed legs.

She was still fuming when the pair got off the bus, three blocks from Cathy's house.

"I even had my schedule changed so my study periods were the same as yours. What's the use of that now? It seems to me you might have stood up for me more than you did, since I went to such trouble for you. But no, you just sat there."

Cathy slapped her feet down hard as the damp of another disregarded puddle seeped through her shoes. The heat of her temper was fast rising to where it canceled the danger of taking cold from wet feet—and there was a certain degree of satisfaction in the knowledge that she was spattering Joan as liberally as herself. "I couldn't bear to interrupt that noble bit about dropping from an A to a B in a worthy cause. Besides, it didn't occur to me that you needed standing up for. I thought you and Miss Vincent always got along fine."

"Well, I didn't do it by apple polishing like you were," Joan said bitingly, then proclaimed in a mincing, goody-goody voice, "Yes, Miss Vincent. You're right, Miss Vincent. Thank you, Miss Vincent."

"Oh, Joan, for heaven's sake!" Cathy cried, exasperated. "You sound like a five-year-old. What did you expect me to do, call her names? And anyway, I think she's probably right. It won't kill you to have time to do some of your own studying at school, and it might be better for both of us to be apart once in a while."

She realized that this was not the most tactful phrasing she could have thought of if she really wanted to smooth Joan's ruffled feathers, but, deep down, she didn't really care whether she managed that or not.

"All right, then!" Joan snatched her arm from Cathy's and lunged out of reach. "If that's how you feel, *be* apart. Walk home by yourself. Let's see how much you don't need me."

Cathy had an instant of blank astonishment, but her spirit was equal to the situation. "All right, I will."

Head high, back erect as a flag pole, she stalked on without slowing her pace. She couldn't hear any footsteps, but she had no doubts that Joan was following close behind, possibly on tiptoe. Her right foot struck the grassy edge of a lawn, and she veered slightly to correct her direction. Presently it was her left foot that sank into the spongy grass. If she had been less angry or less aware of the jeering eyes probing into her from the rear, she could have steered a straighter course, but now cutting her speed in half and gritting her teeth in concentration proved of small value. The left foot was soon cushioned by grass again. Once more she swerved to the middle of the sidewalk, and for a space there was nothing but pavement under her shoe soles.

A snicker burst from Joan, revealing that she was indeed not many steps behind. "You're starting up somebody's driveway. You should just see yourself, the way you stagger! It is too funny for words." She ran forward and grasped Cathy's elbow. "Come on, I'll lead you."

Cathy shook her off. "Never mind. I'll get home by myself."

With extreme dignity, she turned and, guided by the wet swish of a passing car, walked deliberately across the cool, fresh-smelling grass of the terrace to the edge of the road. There she spread the skirt of her rain coat and gracefully seated herself on the curb. She was quite confident that she could find her way home alone from here. This was familiar territory, and the streets were fairly quiet at this hour, but she was not going to stumble or wobble a step farther for the benefit of Joan's warped sense of humor.

"What did you do that for?" Joan asked, her amusement sliding to uneasiness. "Come on. Let's go."

"I am very comfortable here, thank you," Cathy said coldly. "You go on, though. My mother will be calling yours in another ten minutes to find out why I'm not home yet, and she'll be launching a full-scale search if you aren't there to explain that there's nothing to worry about."

"Cathy, don't be silly. Can't you take a joke?" Joan's shoes scraped to and fro on the sidewalk without getting anywhere. "Come on. Stand up, and let's go."

Cathy ignored her. A fleck of rain struck her cheek. A second drop landed on her head. She unfolded her plastic kerchief and proceeded to tie it on.

"It's raining!" Joan's patronizing air melted like salt at the discovery. She swooped across the narrow strip of grass and hunched down beside Cathy, a hand hovering on Cathy's arm. "Come on, please. I was only teasing you. I'm sorry. You know I wouldn't leave you to walk alone. I couldn't. Come on, Cathy. Please."

"Well—" Cathy yielded and unhurriedly returned to the sidewalk and the eager guidance of Joan's arm. She had been more nervous there on the curb than she liked to admit to herself, familiar territory or no. These past few minutes had conjured up shades of Earl Lee and the railroad depot that were not pleasant to contemplate.

She was silent through the two-and-a-half-block flow of Joan's apologies and light chatter designed for peacemaking. Not until they turned in at her own front walk, did she say, "Never mind. I'm not mad any more." Then, her fingers arched on the chilly, rain-speckled handle of the door, she delivered her parting shot. "I'll see you Monday—at the bus stop. I'm taking Trudy."

9

THE TIPS of Cathy's extended fingers just touched the surface of the microphone—and drew back. It was right where she thought it was. She sucked in a deep but soundless breath and began:

"I am Cathy Wheeler, and I want to explain to you about a new member of the student body you'll be seeing in the halls and some of the classrooms from now on. She is my guide dog, Trudy. She is a very gentle dog and won't harm anybody, but she is here to do a special job, so I am asking you please not to distract her by whistling or calling her or patting her as she goes by or doing anything else that might take her mind off what she is supposed to be doing. We will both appreciate it. Thank you."

She nodded to the student announcer waiting at her right and stepped aside to show him she was finished. He struck the *do-re-fa-do* chimes that signed off each broadcast on the school public address system, clicked a switch, and the faint hum of the loud-speaker in the outer office vanished. Introducing Trudy into the routine of Wilson High was as simple as that.

"You did very well, Cathy," said Mr. Yager, the principal. They were in his private office, where the broadcasting apparatus was set up in order that his daily message to the school might be made more conveniently. "If you or Trudy run into any problems, don't hesitate to come to me. However, I'm sure Trudy isn't going to have many difficulties."

"I don't know about that," said the boy who was the announcer. "It won't be such an easy thing to resist petting that dog. Boy, she's a beauty!"

Cathy smiled at him, more pleased by the compliment than if it were aimed at her. "You're welcome to pet her now. It's only when she's working, or under orders to sit or lie still, that I don't like her to be disturbed." She stooped to run her own hand the length of Trudy's lean body. The dog was sprawled flat on the carpet, as comfortably as though Monday mornings in the principal's office were a commonplace affair. "Trudy, will you shake hands?"

Trudy sat up quickly and offered a paw first to Mr. Yager, and next to the boy, who was already on his knees beside her.

"Now, then," Mr. Yager said, "can Trudy find her way to your homeroom, or would you like some help?"

Before Cathy could answer, Trudy's new friend said, "I'll walk back with them, sir."

"Thank you," Cathy said to him and to Mr. Yager together. The truth was that she had no clearer idea of the floor plan of the school now than she did on her first day here, and, of course, unless she could direct Trudy which way to go and where to stop, they were both helpless. But she was reluctant to admit this in front of strangers, especially when one was the principal.

She reached for Trudy's harness and thankfully followed the footsteps of their escort through the door, saying, "We're in 205."

"Right. I thought I'd seen you around there a couple of times last week," he told her. As they passed through the outer office and into the hall, he added, "By the way, my name is Steve Hubert. I don't remember whether I mentioned it at the start of the broadcast or not. I was supposed to."

Cathy laughed. "I don't remember either. I think maybe you did, but I was too nervous to listen. I never had to talk into a microphone before."

"Nobody would have guessed it to hear you," Steve said. "You did fine. I've done plenty of talking on my brother's tape recorder, and the tin-can-on-a-stick kind of mikes my buddy and I used to make when we were little, but today was my first try on the air, too. You have to be at least a junior to qualify for student announcer, and then they pick five of us, so it works out that each announcer gets to do one week in every five. Today was my first shot at it, and if you think you were nervous——"

They chuckled in sympathy, but they might have been as silent as the rows of lockers that lined the walls for all the notice Trudy took of them. A barely perceptible tremor of the leash told that she was glancing from side to side now and again, missing nothing of her new surroundings, but she trotted along at her usual brisk pace and mounted the stairs to the second floor as confidently as though she had been doing it for years. Then, a quarter of the way down the hall, she suddenly slowed, hesitating as if she expected a fresh command of some sort.

"Trudy," Cathy asked, surprised, "what's the trouble?"

"She's wondering if you want to go in here. This is 205. How about that!" Although Steve was speaking low, so as not to disturb the rooms opening onto the empty, echoing hall, his amazement was plain.

Cathy was hardly less astounded. "She has only been here once. I stopped in here for about five minutes to explain to Mrs. Scott that I had to go down to the principal's office this morning. That's all." She bent and hugged Trudy, regardless of what Steve or anyone else who might happen to observe her would think. "Good girl, Trudy. You're a good girl!"

"She knows it. Look at her tail go!" Steve exclaimed. "Say, Cathy, I'd like to do a story on you two. I'm an assistant editor on the Wilson *Times*, and I'm a lot better reporter than announcer, I promise you. The interview wouldn't be for a few weeks yet, but it would make a great story, if it's O.K. with you."

"Well, if you want to. Fine," Cathy agreed. "Any time."

She could not help being flattered, the same as she could not help liking him. If his appearance measured up at all to his voice, he must be close to handsome, for, although his voice was soft, it was firm and clear cut, and there was an element of self-assurance beneath its friendliness that suggested he had no fears about being able to stand on his own two feet.

Nevertheless, she was not sorry when he left her at her homeroom seat and went off into the hall again, on his way to classes and friends that did not concern her. The peppermint-and-onion tainted memory of Earl

Lee was a blight on her interest in any boy before it even sprouted. She pushed Steve Hubert to the back of her mind, where he was soon forgotten as Trudy's first day in school unfolded.

"Trudy, you're a marvel," Cathy found herself saying over and over, sometimes under her breath, sometimes crooning it into the big, up-curved ears. "You're wonderful!"

And she was. Joan went with Cathy and her dog from class to class, as usual, showing them the routes, but Trudy traveled the crowded halls and stairways like a veteran, not in the least confused or shaken by the throngs of students or the noise. In fact, Cathy caught her gently nudging anybody ahead of them who had a tendency to dawdle, an act which never failed to startle a gasp from the nudgee, but which also speeded up progress so promptly that Cathy pretended to be unaware of what was going on.

What was more, Cathy discovered that her own confusion was fading, too. There wasn't such a tumult in the halls as she had thought, nor such a churning multitude of people struggling in every direction at once. The jumble of turns and staircases and room numbers that were a hopeless labyrinth to her last week began to assume a pattern that was surprisingly simple. It was as if there were a magic in the harness handle, transforming chaos into order.

Trudy was just as much at home in the classrooms as she was in the halls. She snuffed curiously at the legs and under sides of the desks, but a word from Cathy collapsed her comfortably on the floor next to Cathy's feet, and there she stayed, quiet and contented, until the end of the period.

It was the same in the cafeteria, except that Cathy

had to snatch bites and swallow fast to get her lunch eaten between answering questions about Trudy and refusing the quantities of food offered for her, everything from jelly sandwiches to lemon cake. "She has her own food in her own dish once a day," she explained again and again. "That is plenty to keep her in shape. Anything else will only get her fat, or maybe make her sick, and I'm not in favor of either."

"Boys are standing around this table six deep," Joan whispered to her, exultant. "No wonder you wanted to bring that animal."

It sounded so much like a remark Francie or Georgie would make that Cathy took a long sip of milk rather than risk an answer. After all, Joan was being a good sport about Trudy. She referred to her as "that animal," or "that creature," or "your beast" if she couldn't avoid referring to her altogether, but there were no signs of Friday's storm returning. She hadn't even commented this morning when Cathy had produced the square key padlock she had bought at the hardware store over the weekend and snapped it on her locker in place of the original combination lock that had to be opened by someone who could see to dial it.

And now Joan was reaping her reward in the form of boys by the handful, a situation that wasn't leaving her much time for lunch, either. She didn't seem to mind, though. She was trading quips with everyone, tossing off flip replies to questions a mile a minute and laughing more shrilly and excitedly than Cathy had ever heard her do before. The result, Cathy noticed, was that the boys were not lingering long, but drifting off after a comment or two. Joan appeared not to be disturbed by this, however, or else she did not realize it, and Cathy could not see any means of enlightening her without hurting her feelings. As for herself, she cared very little whether the boys stayed or went. She was no more excited about them than she was about the girls who were also stopping to admire Trudy. So, if Joan thought she was having fun, there was nothing to gain by spoiling it for her. Let her enjoy it, and welcome.

Still, this was a new side of Joan that Cathy hadn't suspected. She was wondering why she should be feeling a trifle embarrassed about the revelation when Joan wasn't, and saying for the millionth time, "No, only regular dog food That's plenty," when someone tapped her on the shoulder.

"Hi, Cathy! It's Mary Beth. Mind if I sit down?"

"Hi!" Cathy replied and slid over on the bench, although space at the moment was no problem. Six deep around the table the boys might be, but they were apparently quite willing to stand. "Help yourself. Do you have your grammar for today?"

"Checked and double checked," Mary Beth said cheerfully. She perched herself on the corner of the bench, her back to the table, to keep from rousing Trudy, lying calmly underneath. "But I saw Miss Vincent in the hall this morning. She stopped me before I got to my locker, and that's what I want to talk to you about. Have you settled on anybody for your English reader yet?"

Cathy hesitated. Joan's elbow dug into her ribs, but an ear-piercing giggle told that her companion was not only looking in another direction, but that her attention was glued to another conversation.

Cathy grinned, relieved. "Nobody yet. Are you volunteering?"

"If you think I can do it," Mary Beth said. "Miss

Vincent wasn't terribly flattering. She said she thought it would do me good to be obliged to study. But I think it would be fun to study together, and I asked her to let me have a chance to talk to you first, before she mentions it to whoever else she has in mind."

Cathy's grin widened. Here was somebody who wasn't prepared to sacrifice nobly on her behalf, but was hoping to get as much out of reading for her as she did. She crumpled up her sandwich wrapper and thrust it into her bag. "If you have second, fourth, or seventh hour free, we're in business."

Mary Beth had second hour, and she was under the table, paying her respects to Trudy, the bargain sealed, by the time Joan turned to see what other prospects for conversation there were.

From that day on, Miss Vincent had no further cause for disapproving of Cathy on the score that she was always with just one girl. Mary Beth had more friends than she could count, and a large share of them quickly became Cathy's as well. Instead of eating their lunches in an isolated corner of the cafeteria, where they had no company but latecomers who could find no other place to sit, she and Joan became members of a table that was alive with chatter and laughing and half serious discussions that left out no one who wanted to be included.

"Most of them are just freshman," Joan objected once on the way home. "I feel like I'm sitting in on a kindergarten sometimes."

But she continued to sit in, all the same, and when the group planned a Friday night movie party or a Sunday afternoon at the roller skating rink, she seldom had more elevated affairs too pressing to allow her to attend. Now and then, Cathy wondered if Joan were actually much entertained by these excursions, for as often as not she spent the time criticising this thing or that, but Cathy was glad to have her along, anyway. Joan had so few friends—practically no real ones—and Cathy was collecting so many that she felt rather guilty about it on the occasions that she left Joan behind.

And Trudy gathered in new friends, too, a circle that broadened every day. By her third week at Wilson, her course through the halls could be followed simply by listening to the chain of, "Hi, Trudy," "Morning, Trudy," "Hello, Trudy," that chimed along her path like individual notes in a Swiss bell-ringing concert. Trudy pretty generally ignored them, but Cathy responded with a nod or smile, or a "Hi," if a belated "Hi, Cathy," were tacked onto the greeting. Among the most faithful of Trudy's friends was Steve Hubert, who paused almost daily at Cathy's locker in the morning to talk a minute or two and give Trudy a pat.

"Cathy," Mary Beth said in an awed tone when she happened to be a witness to one of these encounters at the locker, "do you know who that was? Steve Hubert!"

Cathy stood on tiptoe to capture her Braille slate, which was determined to slide out of reach into the far corner of the top shelf. "Sure. What about it?"

"What about it!" echoed Mary Beth. "Nothing, of course, except that he's tall, dark and handsome, and captain of the swimming team, and you're probably the only girl in school he has ever looked at twice."

"He doesn't look at me. He looks at Trudy." Cathy lunged upward and, managing to get her fingertips on the slate, dragged it forward to where she could clamp a thumb around it, too. "You forgot to mention that he also likes dogs."

"Well, all I know is what I hear from my sister," Mary Beth said, unconvinced. "She says he's *the* unavailable man in the junior class. Not that he's snooty or shy or anything like that, but that's the trouble. He's not the dating kind, but he's so nice about it that she and the rest of the junior girls would have their teeth pulled and strung into necklaces if it would interest him."

Cathy burst into a laugh at the picture this presented. "I bet it would startle him into that second look, anyhow. Maybe I could make a tidy profit by renting Trudy to juniors on slow afternoons."

"Oh, don't try talking men to Cathy," Joan advised, idly juggling the latch of Cathy's locker up and down. "She's a man hater. You know Pete Sheridan, don't you? He's ten times cuter than this Steve, for my money, but she hardly ever speaks to him, even though they live on the same block, only three houses apart."

Cathy shrugged. She tucked the slate inside a notebook and picked up her purse from the floor of the locker. "We don't have anything to speak about."

It was the truth. Pete was frequently on the bus she took in the mornings, and once or twice he had walked home with her and Trudy in the afternoon, but their attempts at conversation had a habit of sagging in the middle. It wasn't that Pete wasn't friendly, or that Cathy was harboring a grudge of any sort. Their old comradeship was gone, though, more dead than if it had never been. Somehow, they had grown into strangers during this past year, like a tree trunk branching out into two trunks halfway up, and no amount of good will on either side would serve to mend the split. They were simply neighbors now, without much more in common than the fact that they lived on the same block. Besides, Pete regarded himself as quite a lady's man these days, and there were enough similarities between his approach and Earl Lee's to make Cathy a trifle sick inside.

"Well, that's life, I suppose," Mary Beth sighed. "Us poor, plain women run around with our tongues lolling out in hopes of a second look, and the women who are wading in second looks to their shoulder blades are men haters. If I had that auburn hair and those dimples and that shape of yours, Cathy, I'd be the choosiest female in town. Maybe not Steve Hubert choosy, though."

"Yes, I've heard how poor, plain Mary Beth stays home alone Saturday nights until as late as seven-thirty or eight." Cathy closed her locker, poked a finger in the coin pocket of her purse to make sure she had her key and snapped the padlock shut. "And I'm not a man hater. It's just that I don't think they're as vital as some other things."

This statement sounded so puffed up and ridiculous that even she couldn't keep a straight face, and there was no resisting Mary Beth's mirth. She hadn't really meant to be funny, though—but she decided it was as well that the girls took it in that fashion. People who had no Burton in their lives and no threat of having to return there crouching ever at their heels, like a specter tiger, ready to pounce at the first sign of failure, could never understand how working for good grades and no failures might be the most important concern in the world—more important than dates or parties or popularity or getting easy teachers and fooling tough ones or planning trips for the next days of vacation or any of the favorite topics among the girls she knew. It was the single candle she had lighted, according to Dr.

Bradson's advice, and, if need be, she was prepared to pour her whole energies into keeping it lit. But the responsibility of carrying it made her feel older than the other girls, sometimes, and less typical than she would like to be.

Joan did her bit to drive this last point home a few weeks later when she and Cathy and Trudy arrived at Cathy's locker in the morning to find Steve already waiting there.

"Remember that story I said I'd like to do on you and Trudy for the *Times?*" he asked. "It's been so long that maybe you've forgotten, but I haven't. There's a perfect spot for it in the next issue, and I was wondering if you could spare me a quarter of an hour or so after school some day this week for an interview?"

Cathy was taken by surprise. She had nearly forgotten, or anyhow had supposed he had. "Of course, I don't mind. Any day you say. Today, if you want. But what kind of story is it going to be?" She dragged Trudy back from a snuffing inspection of a neighboring locker which was open and within convenient reach, by pulling on the leash. "I warn you that it's likely to be pretty dull, though, unless you're interested in printing the sordid details of life, like the fact that Trudy's a snoop, and that she snores in biology class."

"Atta girl, Trudy!" Steve stooped to scratch the dog's ears. "If you have an honest opinion, express it. Why be inhibited?" He stood up. "Today would be great. I'll meet you here after school, and we'll commandeer an empty room somewhere. Don't worry about the story. Just leave that to me."

"No, don't worry," Joan said as soon as he was gone. "I can see the headline now: BLIND GIRL MAKES GOOD. Or: BRAVE BLIND STUDENT

183

SURMOUNTS COUNTLESS OBSTACLES TO ATTAIN INSPIRATIONAL SUCCESS. I bet we'll have to wrap that issue of the paper in a rain coat to get it home, it'll be so full of slush."

"He wouldn't write that sort of stuff. Steve has better sense." Cathy unknotted her head scarf and crammed it into her coat pocket, wishing for the thousandth time that she had used more discretion in airing her resentments and displaying her tender spots to Joan in those early days of their friendship. She believed Joan's perpetual bristlings in defense of blind people were sincere enough, but it seemed that Cathy winced more often from their sting than did the intended targets. "Besides, I haven't made good yet or attained success. I have my fingers crossed so tight at the moment, that I'm not sure I'll be able to type my mid-Semester exams next week. There's nothing inspirational in that."

"Depends on how you write it," Joan insisted. "Think how inspired you'd be to read about a poor, handicapped girl facing the approaching exams with determination and courage. It's bound to be something like that, because he must feel sorry for you himself, or else why would he be doing his part to brighten your dark life by stopping here every day? You know what Mary Beth said about him and girls, and, to be perfectly frank, although you are fairly attractive, there are prettier girls around this school."

"It could be I'm the only one not chasing him," Cathy said shortly and turned her back on Joan, to shrug out of her coat and hang it inside the locker. She was oddly hurt and more than half angry by such a view of Steve's motives, but each piece of evidence she churned to the surface of her mind to prove that Joan was wrong—that Steve was purely a casual friend, that he looked on her as Trudy's owner rather than as a girl, was pleasant and courteous toward everyone— had a double edge that could be flipped as easily to prove Joan was right.

When Cathy sat down in the chair Steve pulled out for her at a vacant reading table in the rear of the library that afternoon, she was on guard against anything he might ask and as nervous as though she were about to have a tooth drilled through to the nerve. At first he did not appear to notice that her answers were only monosyllables, mostly "yes," and "no," but the third time she dropped Trudy's leash on the floor in as many minutes, her thanks for his retrieving it were too stammering to be ignored.

"Come on, loosen up," he urged. "Have you taken the fifth amendment or something? What's the matter? I'm not an investigating committee, you know."

She had to smile. "I'm sorry. It kind of seems like an investigation, though, being interviewed."

"Think how it would be if you were the President!" Steve flipped his notebook shut and pushed it forward on the table. "Let's forget the interview for awhile, then, and talk about something else—Trudy, for instance. What does she do if you have to walk somewhere in the rain?"

Cathy reached a hand down to Trudy, who raised her head at the mention of her name. "She trots along as usual, except a little slower maybe. She doesn't really care for rain or puddles. The funny part of it is that she likes other kinds of water, though—hoses, bathtub faucets, fountains, fish ponds. If there's a sprinkler that happens to be hitting the sidewalk. I have to push her ahead, because she'll stop still in the middle of the spray to admire it."

Steve laughed, leaning to look at Trudy, too. "Have you ever taken her swimming?"

"No, but I think it would be fun. They allow dogs on the lake beach, the north section, don't they? I'd like to go in with her there next summer."

"I'm pretty sure they do." There was a new spark of interest in Steve's voice. "Do you swim?"

Cathy straightened in her chair, her interest also kindling. "I used to, but I haven't been in the water for over a year. Now I'm waiting for next year and warm weather. You get to swim the year round, being captain of the team and all, don't you?"

Steve agreed, but he was less enthusiastic about tank swimming than he was about lakes or natural pools. They began comparing notes on their favorite swimming spots, and then on places where they had gone skating or hiking or bicycle riding. From there the talk gradually drifted to movies, and on to music and to record players, until a bell rang suddenly throughout the building, cutting them short.

"Four o'clock already?" Steve exclaimed, incredulous. "It can't be. I've kept you here practically an hour, and I told you this morning it wouldn't take more than fifteen minutes."

"That's all right." Cathy reached out for Trudy, who, grown wise in the language of bells, was getting to her feet and stretching, sure that they had been dismissed. "There's always another bus coming. It doesn't seem as if it has been more than fifteen minutes, anyway. Are you positive that's the four o'clock bell?"

"Positive. Actually, it's ten past four, according to my watch." He stood up, riffling the pages of his notebook. "Never mind the bus tonight. I have my dad's car here, and I'll give you a ride home. It's a little extra service the *Times* provides in appreciation of co-operative interviewees."

"But you didn't get an interview," Cathy protested as he held her coat for her. "We didn't ever get back to it. In fact, I almost did forget that was what we were here for."

"Well—" Steve cleared his throat rather sheepishly. "I scribbled down a few notes here and there while we were talking. Silent ball point pen, you know."

Cathy twisted around to face him, uncertain whether to yield to dismay at having been fooled into lowering her guard, after all, or to disappointment that the whole, lively discussion she'd been enjoying was strictly a business proposition to him, or to turn it into the laughter that her common sense told her was the only graceful means of preserving her dignity. The laughter won, although not without a sharpening pinch of pepper. "In that case, thanks. I'll accept the ride. But it will serve you right if it turns out that I live miles off the beaten track."

"No extra charge within the city limits," Steve said good-naturedly, and she was glad she'd left unsaid the hotter words that had flitted to the tip of her tongue.

The chill nip of the November evening finished the cooling of Cathy's temper as she walked with Steve to his car. Early as the season was, there was a smell of snow in the air which did not encourage standing on windy bus corners unnecessarily and made the car heater the most welcome of luxuries. It set the two young people to talking of winter and of snow, of sleds and toboggans and fireplaces and bowls of steaming chili until they were both surprised by Trudy's rearing up from her folded position under the dashboard and whining eagerly as her nose came on a level with the windshield.

"Something tells me this must be the place," Steve said, pulling in to the curb. "The address checks, the porch light's on, and Trudy seems to have an attachment for it. But this isn't what I'd call 'miles off the beaten track.' "

Cathy laughed, opening the door and letting Trudy scramble out. "I decided to forgive you and move closer in to town."

Steve came around the car to help her out and walk beside her to the house. "You've decided I'm trustworthy now?" he asked.

Cathy felt her face redden, but she glossed over it with another laugh and gave him the truth. "No, I'm not deciding on that until I see your story in print."

Still, this was not quite the truth. Although she did continue to have Joan-inspired reservations about the wisdom of letting herself be written up in the school paper, nevertheless, when the next issue of the *Times* was finally distributed in the homerooms, the excitement with which she received her copy was born as much of anticipation as misgivings.

"Here it is in the 'Personalities' column, in fact, it's the whole column," Joan said, drawing Cathy into a corner the first chance she had. "Brace yourself. Here goes:

"For those of you who have been noticing that the freshmen are coming in pairs this year, allow us to introduce you to the most outstanding team, Cathy Wheeler and Trudy. Trudy is the one with a passion for lawn sprinklers and bubbling fountains. Cathy is the one with the freckles and the smile. . . ."

As she listened, Cathy did become the one with the smile, but if the freckles were visible, she knew they must be at least toned down for the moment by a general, self-conscious pink that was warming her skin. Steve had woven the article of little more than the ordinary, run-of-the-mill things they had talked about that day and other days before, but he had done it in such a way that they sounded fresh and different and attractive. Part of the story was light, part rather on the serious side, but nowhere in it was there a bid for sympathy, and not once did he use the words *blind*, or *handicapped,* or the hackneyed *inspirational*. It wasn't that he tried to hide the fact that she couldn't see; he just accepted it as nothing very remarkable, and went on to report the positive things about her.

"Well, you can't say Steve didn't give enough space to the dog. It has a full quarter of the column," was the worst Joan could accuse him of.

Cathy did not pretend to be critical. "I wouldn't change a letter of it," she told Steve when he coughed significantly behind her as she was piling notebooks on her locker shelf at the end of the day. "Not even the freckles. I've been feeling famous ever since I read it."

"Whew!" he exclaimed. "That's a relief. I wasn't sure I dared approach close enough to ask you what you thought. Trudy might have had orders to attack on sight. When your name goes up in lights on Broadway, remember the guy who started you off. And the freckles were the best part. Ask Mr. Simms, the *Times* advisor."

There was no opportunity to argue, for he was due at swimming practice immediately and couldn't stay to talk.

"Hello, Steve! Congratulations on a marvelous article," Joan called from her locker on the opposite side of the hall. It was her high, too shrill, come-hither voice but it shifted to a sour mutter as she joined Cathy a minute later. "My, my, but don't we have the big shots around here. It's evidently beneath their dignity to acknowledge a greeting, let alone a compliment."

"Probably he didn't hear you," Cathy said. "He was in a hurry to be downstairs."

"You're so right, he didn't hear me," Joan said bitterly, "or see me or anything me. You might think no woman existed around here but you, and I'll bet you won't be seeing much of him either any more, now that he has his good deed done for the year. Unless, of course, you can produce some other kind of qualification to appeal to the boy scout reporter in him."

Cathy's brows drew together. "You don't know a thing about it." She had an impulse to shoot out a fire of words that would scorch Joan to silence, once and for all, but the sound of Miss Vincent up the hall, scolding a luckless student for noisiness, caused her to think twice, and the moment passed.

And for a while, it seemed that Joan's prediction was not as ill-founded as it might have been. Twice in the next few days, Cathy came to school early, to work with Mary Beth on a panel discussion of *David Copperfield,* which meant she was elsewhere at the time Steve usually passed her locker, and, the following week, it was his turn to announce on the morning PA broadcasts, which meant he was the one to arrive early and to be busy until class time.

Cathy was surprised at how much she missed him, and at how happy she was to accept when he made a special point of cornering her between classes the day before Thanksgiving, to offer her another ride home.

But that was nothing to her delighted astonishment the week after Thanksgiving when he asked, "Do you suppose Trudy could weather the blow if you left her alone for an evening and went to the Press Club dance with me?"

"Oh, Cathy!" Mary Beth squealed when Cathy broke the news to the girls at lunch. "The big Christmas dance! If Tony doesn't ask me now, I'll shoot him. Naturally, you said you'd go?"

"Need you ask? Look at the grin on her," said Ruth Meyer from across the table. "What became of those famous last words about more vital things than boys in life? Are they staying home with Trudy?"

Cathy wrinkled her nose at the friendly teaser, but her grin would not be concealed. "It's Christmas, and a person has to have a little fun. Besides, I wouldn't go with just anybody for the sake of going, but Steve is different."

There was a gratifying chorus of agreement the length of the table, but Joan's voice rose above the rest. "You mean *you* are different. He wouldn't stoop to asking an ordinary girl that nobody'd stare at or admire him for inviting."

The table was instantly as silent as though a hand had been clapped over every mouth. Cathy's elation vanished like a blown-out flame. Never before had Joan delivered one of these humiliating shots in the presence of an audience.

Slowly and very distinctly, Ruth said, "That is the nastiest thing I ever heard you say, Joan Norton. And I've heard you say plenty."

Cathy's nails dug into the palm of her left hand, lying clenched in her lap. "I don't think she meant it

191

the way it sounds," she said, more in an effort to change the subject than to defend Joan.

"I don't care how she meant it," Ruth said, "there was no excuse for saying such a thing. And I think she does mean it. She's green jealous of anything nice that happens to somebody else, unless she can take the credit for it, and I'm fed up to my eyebrows with her sneering at everything that's said or done without her special blessing. I would have said this long ago, Cathy, but I thought until today that she was your friend."

"I'm more of her friend than you are," Joan retorted, unquelled. "You're not sticking up for Cathy. You're sticking up for hard-to-get Steve, the boy wonder of Wilson High. Well, I'll bet you whatever you please that he wouldn't be going to that dance if he didn't think it would add to his boy-wonder reputation, and that he'd back out on the deal even now, if a chance at something he liked better should come along."

"Like you, I suppose?" challenged Shirley Macdonald from the farther end of the table.

"It could be," Joan said swiftly. "It could be anybody who flattered his ego by seeming helpless and sweet like Cathy. But I don't have to go around stealing other people's dates. And I don't go around boasting because I've snapped up the first one that offered, either."

"Joan," said Mary Beth coldly, "if we're crowding you, please feel free to eat your sandwiches at another table. I'm sure it will be a help to everyone's digestion."

Joan was already cramming papers into her lunch bag with a fury that rammed elbows and shoulders into Cathy, who was beside her. "This is a public school, and a public school cafeteria, and I have a right to eat wherever I choose. But don't worry." She flung herself off the bench, adding a lunge of her knees to the blows Cathy was receiving. "I wouldn't sit here again if I had to stand up the rest of my life!"

There were tears in her voice, but whether of rage or hurt, Cathy didn't know, and, like Ruth, she didn't much care. It seemed to her burning ears that every word of the past few minutes had been trumpeted through the cafeteria like a proclamation. She wondered that an electrified hush hadn't fallen over the whole room, but the ordinary cafeteria noises were flowing on unaltered, even at the nearest tables—the buzz of voices, the rustle of papers, bursts of guffaws from a group of boys, the clink of pop bottles, the scrape of benches being moved, cascades of soprano giggles. Only her table was momentarily still.

"Well," said Mary Beth finally in an odd, flat tone, "that's that, I guess."

Ruth snorted. "She'll be back. She doesn't have that much pride, more's the pity. But listen, Cathy, if you need new readers after this, if she thinks she'll quit and leave you stranded, we'll pitch in and fill the gap. Just say the word."

"Thanks," Cathy said. She was rewrapping the second half of her sandwich, for she was no longer hungry. Neither was she anxious to dwell on the quarrel, but she smiled her welcome of Ruth's loyalty. "I'll keep you top on the list."

But Joan did not quit. She was seated and waiting that afternoon when Cathy entered the empty room allotted to them for studying. By tacit accord, neither of them referred to the incident at lunch, and if the atmosphere during that hour was cool and wary, the reading was the more business-like and precise. It was a narrow bridge across the split that gaped between

193

them, but, as the days wore on, each for her own reasons was careful not to shake it, and it continued to stand. True to Ruth's prediction, Joan returned to her place at the usual lunch table less than a week later as if nothing had happened, and, since nobody protested or even paid any heed at all to her, she stayed. She was subdued and inclined to be sullenly reserved, but, apparently, she was defeated.

She had her triumph, though, in the shape of a telephone call three days before the dance. Cathy was at her typewriter, elbows planted on the desk, her chin propped on her fists, straining to compose the descriptive essay Miss Vincent had assigned for the Friday class, when she heard the telephone ring and, in another instant, Mark's familiar shout from the foot of the stairs, "Hey, Cathy, it's for you."

She answered on the extension in the upstairs hall, to be greeted by Steve's voice. "How are you fixed for homework, ma'am?" he asked. "Got enough to keep you busy, or might you be in the market for more?"

"No, thanks. I have as much as I can possibly handle," she said firmly, going along with the joke. "Not only am I stocked up for the week, but if I get one more assignment for over the holidays, there won't be any holidays. I may have to lock myself in with the books and throw the key away if I ever hope to get through it."

There was a pause, and the banter dropped from his voice. "I heard you were pretty well loaded down. If you'd rather not pile the dance and a late night on top of it—" He paused again, as if expecting her to answer, but when she did not he went on, "Well, my mother wants to go out of town this weekend, and, since my dad can't get away to drive her, there's nobody but me. I can get out of it, though, if you—"

"No," she cut in quickly. "That's all right." She did not want him to explain further, or to apologize, or to go on pretending that the decision was up to her. "I'm sure I'll survive—with the books."

But when she placed the receiver back in its cradle, she wondered if surviving were worth the effort. She touched a finger to the cold glass of the mirror above the telephone, trying to imagine what was reflected in it that inspired people only to curiosity or pity or gestures of kindness that they later regretted. Certainly she was no movie star, but her hair was getting darker, shading to the auburn she had always coveted, if she were to believe her mother and Grandma Wheeler and Mary Beth. It was curled now, and softly waved, thanks to the home permanent her mother had given her at the start of the semester, and her clothes were fitting her this year in a style that even Francie couldn't call boyish.

Yet there must be something repulsive about her somewhere, something more repelling than just a pair of eyes that couldn't see, for she'd been told they were still outwardly blue and clear and large as new. Or maybe the flaw was in the other people, in the old mistrust of a person who wasn't exactly like them, or in the equally time-polished belief that, because a person wasn't physically perfect outside, she must be either superhuman or subhuman inside and shouldn't or couldn't be treated like other people.

She thought wistfully of the girl who had beamed out at her from this mirror on her fourteenth birthday. That was almost eighteen months ago by calendar reckoning, but she was ages older than that little girl, who hadn't an inkling of what it was to be really disappointed or lonely or too disillusioned for tears.

Her memory full of the other-life birthday, Cathy retraced her steps to the typewriter, and, presently, she was putting into words the never-forgotten picture of sunlight, trees, cliff edge and blue lake under a cloud-frothed sky that she had meant to sketch in pastels that day. For a while she was there again in the small clearing, watching the rushing curve of the whitecaps, smelling the warm sweetness of the tall grass she sat in, feeling the knobbed ridges of twigs pressed into her knees and the hard coolness of pebbles under the heel of her hand, listening to the swish and whisper of waves on the beach below the cliff.

Then the words and the paper came to an end, and, once more, she was shut within the walls of her room, as empty as the typewriter carriage in front of her. Her essay for Friday was done, probably the best she'd ever written, she judged listlessly. Maybe worth an A from Miss Vincent. If nothing else, her single candle was burning strong and steady, and, from now on, she would not swerve her gaze from it. Nevertheless, its flame tonight was cold and cheerless.

10

CHRISTMAS CAME and went, then the last three weeks of the semester, then the nerve-tearing week of final exams, and the exciting, dreaded, longed-for day of judgment was upon Wilson High.

"Why can't they send us our grades in the mail like they do in colleges?" moaned Ruth Meyer, joining Cathy outside the door of the biology room, which was the first class of the day for both of them. "It's plain humiliating to have to stand face to face with a teacher while he's marking the worst on your card. I declare, if Mr. Clark gives me as much as a C in here, I'll name my first child Amoeba out of gratitude."

"Or if it's a boy, you could call it Perry-Mecium," Cathy suggested, although a trifle absently.

She had her own doubts about Mr. Clark's grading. It wasn't that she hadn't spent extra hours studying for the exam or that she hadn't been prepared when she arrived to take it, but Mr. Clark had gone all of a fluster as to how he should administer such an important test. After half an hour's delay while he decided, he placed a chair for her in the hall near his door, and divided the rest of the period between popping in to check on the others of the class and popping out to whisper questions to her and scribble down her whispered answers. It was hardly an atmosphere to induce calm, clear thinking, and when it was over, she found she couldn't remember a thing she had said to him.

Her knees were inclined to be a bit trembly as she sat down at her desk behind Ruth's and fished in her purse for the oblong of cardboard on which the whole tale of her achievements or failures these past five months would be written in ink by the end of the morning. There was one thing to be thankful for, though. This was a short day. The periods were cut to twenty minutes apiece, just long enough for the students to get their cards marked in each class and move on to the next. By noon, the suspense would all be over.

"We'll do this in alphabetical order," Mr. Clark announced when the bell brought a thinning of the nervous buzz that filled the room. "Come up to the desk as soon as you are called, or we won't get through in time. Please try to keep the noise down, too," he added, as though he did not have much faith that anyone actually would try. "Addler . . ."

Cathy opened the Braille magazine she had brought to keep herself occupied and settled down for the long wait that was penalty for being named Wheeler. Her Braille reading speed had increased unbelievably since she had left Burton and had been obliged to study from the notes she took in class, and this magazine, *Braille Book Review*, was one of her favorites. In it were listed the latest and newest books available from the library, in Braille, on talking book records and on tape recordings, plus various notices related to books, and sometimes an author's biography or a review copied from a newspaper. She enjoyed scanning the book titles and reading the three or four lines of synopsis under each, but today her fingers were damp and stuck to the dots, instead of moving smoothly across them. When she did push on to the bottom of a page, she had to go back and re-read it, anyway, for her mind had not registered a single word.

"Wheeler," Mr. Clark said mechanically.

Cathy sprang up as though she had been ejected from a toaster. Startled, Trudy lunged for the door, which was closer than Mr. Clark's desk and, apparently, seemed to her the logical direction in which to head in case of such sudden movements. Cathy had to drag her back by the leash and speak to her twice before they managed to arrive at Mr. Clark's hand, which materialized practically out of nowhere to take the report card from Cathy's.

"You have an A," he murmured, his pen scratching firm, quick strokes. "Congratulations!" He thrust the card into her hand again and said, "Whitman . . ."

Cathy walked on air back to her seat. It was as much as she could do not to laugh aloud at Ruth's stifled squeal when she passed the card forward to her for her inspection. An A! It was more than she had dared to hope for, even before that muddled exam. How had it happened?

Like a green worm wriggling out onto the petal of a perfect rose, Miss Creel's voice slithered from a dark corner of her memory: "Your teachers will pity you, too, and give you high grades, whether you work or not."

"But I did work," Cathy told herself and Miss Creel

fiercely. "I worked hard. I studied my fingers to the bone."

Yet how could she be sure that the results were A quality? She wasn't sure. Ever since the exam, she'd been hoping and praying for nothing lower than a C. But she wasn't sure the exam had been that bad, either. It was Mr. Clark who was trained to be the judge, and anyhow, how would you go about accusing a teacher of unfairness on the grounds that he'd marked you too high on an exam you'd honestly studied to pass?

The first, bright glitter was gone from the A, though. It did not quiet her uneasiness any to have a second unexpected A added to it by Miss O'Brien, her Spanish teacher. Offhand, Cathy could think of several mistakes she'd made on the Spanish exam, although, all in all, it had been simpler than she had expected, and Miss O'Brien, like Mr. Prentice, the algebra teacher, had avoided Mr. Clark's confusion by having her come in early to write the questions for herself in Braille, so that she could answer them unmolested at a typewriter in another room. Until now, however, A's had been sprinkled too thinly through her school life for her to be quite convinced that only a little extra work and serious studying could be altogether responsible for such a shower of them. How much it really troubled her, she did not realize, though, until Mr. Prentice knocked the weight of it from her shoulders in his room as he recorded her algebra grade on the card.

"You just squeaked in under the wire, Cathy, but you made it. It's a B."

She had been almost positive she did better than "just squeaking in under the wire" on his exam, but here was proof that one teacher, at any rate, was not giving her anything out of the kindness of his heart.

Her relief was stronger than her disappointment, and she had a wild impulse to hug him. As it was, the smile with which she delivered her "Thank you" must have caused him to think she'd been prepared for him to fail her.

Then she was on her way to Miss Vincent's class and the final, acid test. True to her declaration at the start of the semester, Miss Vincent never played favorites. She had placed her typewriter on a table in the front of the room for the exam, and there Cathy had typed her answers to the questions Miss Vincent dictated in a half whisper, while the rest of the class wrote their answers to mimeographed copies of the same questions at their desks. Whatever grades Miss Vincent was waiting to bestow would be coldly calculated on the basis of merit alone, a prospect that Cathy found hardly more attractive, now that the moment was here, than that of A's for charity.

"But everybody says she's fair," she told Mary Beth in an effort to reassure them both as they walked toward the room. "She was pretty fair on the mid-semester exam, I thought."

"Deadly fair," Mary Beth agreed hollowly. "That's what I'm scared of. I don't think I did too badly on the exam, but whenever I think like that, it's a sure sign I've dropped twenty points."

Miss Vincent's greeting to the class was scarcely designed to inspire more confidence. "Any of you who wishes to see his examination grade may stop here at the desk after the period, but if I were some of you, I would not admit I had even put my name to such a paper. All I can say is that it is fortunate for a number of you that the grade for the whole semester does not depend entirely on your showing in the examination."

Cathy did not even pretend to read away the space between Archer and Wheeler this time. The magazine lay flat and shut on her desk, and ever conscious of Miss Vincent's aversion to fidgeting, she rested tightly clasped hands on it to hold them still. A dusty smell of chalk floated in the air and a sharp odor of moth balls, as though somebody, perhaps Miss Vincent, were wearing clothes just taken from storage. There was an unnatural quiet like a pent-in breath quivering from wall to wall, except for Trudy, who had caught the general nervousness and was whining softly to herself, but staying put as rigidly as Cathy.

Name by name, Miss Vincent summoned the students to her desk, and, one by one, they marched up and back without a mutter of comment. Two or three of the boys clumped loudly on feet that sounded like leaden-heeled blocks of wood, but most of the class seemed almost to be tiptoeing. Cathy's heart squeezed in on itself, and her muscles tensed as she listened to the feet that responded cautiously to the name Trezise, for Wheeler would be next.

Miss Vincent interrupted her in the act of gathering up Trudy's leash. "Sit where you are, Catherine. I'll mark your card there." As she spoke, she was at Cathy's desk, drawing the card toward her. Without lowering her voice in the slightest, she continued, "I owe you an apology, and the whole class might as well hear it. When I first learned that you were coming to Wilson, I was very much opposed to having you in my class. I thought it was an imposition on me, and that you had no business in a public school, but you have changed my mind completely. It has been a genuine pleasure to have you this semester, and I am only sorry that I'm losing you to Miss Palmer's sophomore English."

For a long second, Cathy was too stunned to smile. She could not have told whether she was more embarrassed or astounded at this public recognition, or whether, perhaps, she just wasn't geared to absorb such a radiant, unlooked-for compliment except by slow, careful degrees.

"Thank you," she heard herself saying dazedly. Then, to add to her confusion, applause began to spatter around her, starting in Mary Beth's corner and sweeping on row by row, like wind-blown rain.

The dismissal bell finally whirred to her rescue, transforming the applause instantly into a book-slamming, foot-stamping, talk-swelling stampede for the door.

"I have something more to discuss with you, Catherine," Miss Vincent said, speaking for once above the din, instead of glaring it down. "It won't take a minute. You aren't in a hurry, are you?"

Cathy shook her head and wound her right arm around Trudy's middle, to pull her close to the desk, where she would not be in danger of getting stepped on or knocked over by assuming her usual after-class position of standing broadside in the aisle.

"Now, then," Miss Vincent said when the room was empty, "I have a message for you from Mr. Simms, who is the advisor for the Wilson *Time*s. I showed him that descriptive theme you wrote about the cliff trail above the lake, and he was very impressed. He wants to know if you would be interested in working on the *Time*s as a member of the staff."

Cathy's encircling arm tightened so quickly that Trudy grunted. She wanted to say yes without hesitation, but a fleeting recollection of Steve Hubert, who also was a member of the *Times* staff, cooled her enthusiasm to a half doubtful, "If you think I could do it."

"Of course I think you can do it." Miss Vincent as a champion was scarcely less snappish than Miss Vincent, classroom terror. "You are a sophomore now, aren't you? That's the main qualification. You are the type of person who will make a success of whatever you determine to do. I know your kind. You'll be editor-in-chief by your senior year, if the job appeals to you, and you'll probably be one of the best editors the *Times* ever had."

It had the ring of an order rather than a prophecy, and Cathy had to laugh to ease the tension. She had read that an overturned lantern caused the great Chicago fire, but that seemed like peanuts compared to the blaze Miss Vincent was expecting her to light from the flame of one small, private candle. "I don't know anything about journalism," she hedged. "I do like English, though, and I like to write things and—" Suddenly, she flung caution to the winds. "Yes, I'd love to have a chance to work on the paper."

"Good!" Miss Vincent said. "I'll tell Mr. Simms, and he will be talking to you about it as soon as the new semester begins. That's next Wednesday, isn't it? A week from today. Congratulations, Catherine, and have yourself a pleasant vacation between semesters."

What Cathy replied, or how she got into the hall, were lost to her in a shining haze of rainbow colors that nothing penetrated until she was abruptly choking for breath in a hug that was threatening to throttle her.

"An A!" Mary Beth was trilling in her ear. "Can you imagine? She gave me an A. I never had one before in English in all my life! I wasn't surprised at your getting one from her, but me—!"

Cathy struggled free, laughing and dizzy and gasping for air. "You might have guessed it when she picked you for a reader. But I'm not sure what she marked me. She forgot to mention it."

"An A, of course," Mary Beth said. "Let's see." She took hold briefly of the edge of the card Cathy extended and sighed. "Sure enough, A in English, as well as Spanish and biology, and a B in algebra. Oh, Cathy! Don't you have any other classes I could add to reading for English, so that maybe some more of this might rub off on me?"

Cathy tucked the precious card into her purse and fastened the clasp. "I don't know about the rubbing off part. I feel like I must have been eating lucky pills for breakfast, but if you're serious, you can have your pick of ancient history or geometry. Ruth wants to do the Spanish. She arranged her schedule especially so we'd be in the same class."

"I'll take either or both, depending on how our schedules match up," Mary Beth said promptly, as they began strolling along the hall in the direction of their lockers. "I have to read the assignments for myself, anyway, and I guess if I read them aloud, I don't skip anything. But what about— Oh, oh, here she comes!"

Cathy did not have to ask who *she* would be. Mary Beth's flattened tone was as revealing as was Joan's own voice, which cooed to meet them in advance of her approaching footsteps. "Hi, girls! Did you pass everything?"

"You could call it that," Mary Beth answered. "What about you?"

Joan's laugh dismissed this as too obvious to require words. "On your way home, Cathy? I notice Pete Sheridan hasn't left yet, so maybe if we hurry, we can all get the same bus."

"Sorry," Cathy replied, "but I'm eating lunch here, and then I'm going on downtown. I have a check-up appointment with the doctor, and my father's bringing me home afterward."

"Well, I've heard of kids who needed a doctor after their fathers saw their report cards, but you're the first one I've heard of who had the foresight to make an appointment in advance," Joan observed in the too-amused voice that so often had the effect of suggesting she was not far from being in earnest. "Oops, there's Pete on the stairs! I'll see you."

"Happy hunting," Mary Beth called after her, then muttered, "Darn, I wanted to flash my A under her nose, and you should have told her what Miss Vincent said to you about the *Times*. I will if you don't want to, because I was looking for my fountain pen that had rolled onto the floor and I heard what she said. I made a noise to let her know I was there, but she just nodded at me in what was practically a friendly way. *That* held me spellbound, to say nothing of my curiosity! I think Joan ought to be the first to know."

Cathy shrugged. "She wouldn't be terribly impressed."

Inwardly she was relieved that neither the subject of the *Times* nor of readers for next semester had been mentioned in Joan's presence. She felt sneaking and underhanded, lining up readers for her new classes before telling Joan their partnership was ended, but she had no intention of signing up as a captive for Joan's "friendship" arrows for another five months, and experience had taught her the safest method for dealing with Joan was to present her with an accomplished fact. As for her appointment to the *Times*, that was still too fresh and bright and wonderful for her to bear having its sheen dimmed by whatever acid-dipped remark Joan was bound to offer by way of congratulation. Most especially, Cathy did not care to hear any remarks concerning Steve Hubert.

In spite of such thoughts, however, she could not help being in a kindly mood toward everyone this day. She even wondered if she weren't a trifle hard on Joan as Trudy and she struck out for the bus stop after lunch. It was such a lovely world, it didn't seem possible that it contained anything but lovely people.

Big, feathery flakes of snow were falling, fluttering against her cheeks or hanging heavily on her eyelashes, one of her favorite kinds of weather. There was no wind, but the flakes made a barely audible, velvet-on-velvet whisper as they fell that ringed her in like a quiet curtain, softening and muffling and blotting out the ordinary sounds of the street. Without Trudy, she would have been uneasy or even afraid, for the regular landmarks by which her ears judged direction and distance were either gone or distorted beyond recognition—the noise of traffic on the boulevard ahead; the echo of her own boots from the walls of houses and buildings; the almost imperceptible change in sound waves that told her more by a feeling than a sound when she was passing a tree or a pole. But with Trudy padding along at her side, calm and competent, she was as relaxed and carefree as the snow itself.

Her luck was still bubbling high when she reached the bus stop, for Trudy had just time to snap once or twice at the snowflakes drifting by her nose before the bus wheezed to a halt at the curb, and its door flopped open. "Downtown, miss," the driver called.

"Thank you." Cathy smiled and followed Trudy

aboard. She dropped her ticket in the fare box with a confidence born of five months' practice. "Will you tell me when we get to Water Street, please?"

"Water Street? Sure thing." The driver flipped the door shut. "There's a seat right behind me."

Cathy thanked him and sank onto the smooth, leather-covered seat he suggested. Trudy took up her customary station, leaning against Cathy's knees. Cathy pulled off her glove, and touched the tiny knob at the side of her wristwatch which released its spring-hinged crystal and sent it flipping up like the top of a jack-in-the-box. The watch was a Christmas present from her parents. On the exposed dial, two Braille dots marked the twelve, and one dot indicated each of the other eleven numbers, so that a finger tip brushed across the hands was enough to show her she had forty-five minutes yet before she was due at Dr. Kruger's office.

She settled back as the bus rumbled on to the next stop . . . and to the next. There was no great hurry as far as she was concerned, and the warmth inside the bus after her walk in the January snow expanded a comfortable drowsiness through her.

"Hi, Cathy!" a voice broke in on her laziness at the third halt of the bus. "What are you doing here?" It was Pete.

"Hi!" she replied, surprised into coming wide-awake again. "I have an appointment downtown. But what are you doing here?"

"I went out for pizza with some of the guys, and now I'm going down to the YMCA to watch a couple of films they're showing this afternoon." He sat down beside her.

"Poor Joan!" Cathy couldn't resist saying. "She was

sure she was going to have the pleasure of your company on the way home."

"Never!" Pete asserted so eloquently that it was hardly necessary for him to add, "Not if I see her first. What's she got, anyway? A haunting license?"

Cathy tried to look innocent, for Joan's sake, but it was impossible not to laugh. "It could be she likes you."

"She'd like a hobbyhorse if you painted BOY on it," Pete said bitterly. "I'll pick my own girls, and you can tell her it won't be one that grabs you by the shirt button and says, 'Have you heard about your date? She can't go to the dance with you, but I can, so you don't have to worry about wasting the tickets.' "

His falsetto imitation of a girl was too funny to ignore, but Cathy's shock was none the less genuine. "You're making that up! She wouldn't really do a thing like that. Nobody would."

"Oh, wouldn't she? Ask Steve Hubert. He was sweating bullets around Christmas time, trying to find excuses not to take her. He finally had to give her a flat no."

An electric spark leaped through Cathy's pulse. "Not to take her where?" she asked carefully.

"The Christmas dance, the big one the Press Club sponsors. Joan got word about his date being canceled before he did. Hey, now that I think of it—" Pete paused to search his memory as the bus lurched around a corner. "Sure! Steve had a date set up with you for that dance, didn't he? But your folks made you break it or were going to make you break it at the last minute because you had such a pile of homework stacked up that you couldn't go anywhere until you finished it, or some such reason. You must know all about it."

"You seem to know much more than I do," Cathy

said. She bent forward on the pretense of assuring herself that Trudy's tail was not lying in the aisle where a careless passenger might step on it. "Only, I didn't break the date. It was Steve."

Pete yawned. "Yeah? I thought it was you, or that you were supposed to be looking for a painless way to do it, or something. I don't know. I got that secondhand from some fellows who heard her talking to Steve, but the part about Joan is true. Everybody was pitching in to help him escape." He laughed suddenly. "Hey, if he shows up at the Y this afternoon, will I have fun prodding him about breaking the first date himself and falling flat in his own trap. Why'd he do it?"

"I don't know," Cathy answered vaguely. "The wires got crossed somewhere, I guess."

That wasn't far wrong, she reflected, thinking back to the night of Steve's telephone call. He must have been scouting for the truth of this homework story, and when she seemed to confirm it, he had offered her an easy way out of the responsibility of leaving him stranded with a pair of rather expensive tickets. If only she hadn't treated his question as a joke, or else, if she had just been a little less quick to believe herself rejected. But both she and Steve, apparently, had been well conditioned in advance for jumping to conclusions in opposite directions.

"He doesn't think I had anything to do with sicking Joan on him, does he?" she asked.

"Search me." Pete yawned again and slumped lower on the seat. "I guess he figured you weren't strong against it. Anyhow, he was plenty mad about the whole thing."

He sounded as if he were rapidly losing interest in the subject, however, and Cathy didn't urge him to say more. What was the use, when the damage was already done, and had been done for quite a spell? Since Steve's call so many weeks ago, he hadn't been near her locker once, as far as she was aware, and on the one or two occasions when they had encountered each other accidentally at the candy counter, their conversation had been limited to a "Hi," apiece, with a "How's Trudy?" and a "Fine," thrown in for good measure. It was too late for the facts to matter much now, except as a possible salve for her wounded pride, but at this moment, she was not sure the cure was not worse than the disease. As for Joan— If it were any time but this afternoon, Cathy would have been seething, but today she was having trouble holding her whole mind to any one thing, and Joan was hardly more than a name crossed off a mental list.

"Here's the Y," Pete said. He stretched up and pulled the buzzer, releasing the cord with a snap. "I'll see you around."

"Yes," Cathy replied, "I'll see you."

The words were as automatic as "So long," or "Goodby," but they sent another electric pulse through her. What if this once they were to prove prophetic? She'd been refusing to think of that all morning, because the merest speculation on it was so thrilling it almost made her ill. But she hadn't been in Dr. Kruger's office for over a year. Who could say what improvements his examination might find today? In spite of her resolution, excitement was mounting in her by leaps and bounds.

"Water Street," the driver called, just as she was wondering if he had forgotten and passed it.

Like an omen of good luck, a soft trio of snowflakes landed on her chin and both eyelids as she and Trudy stepped onto the sidewalk. She knew from the rapid, happy whipping of Trudy's tail that her father was here to meet them as planned, even before he said hello.

"Have you been waiting for us long?" she asked.

"Less than five minutes," he answered and gave her his arm to keep her and Trudy from being separated from him in the downtown crowds. "That's one of the rewards for living right."

Cathy laughed. "I have another one."

She was thinking of her report card, but she had no chance to hand it to him until they were in the elevator, riding up to Dr. Kruger's floor. By then, her heart was pounding so fast that his reaction became only a pleasant blur on the very fringe of her attention.

Walking through the office door was like stepping through the looking glass into the strange-familiar land beyond. Everything was the same as she remembered it from her first visit here, close to two years ago. There was the same sweet-voiced nurse greeting her as she entered, the same springy carpet underfoot, the same loose rattle of the latch as the door swung shut, the same overstuffed chair for her to sit in beside the same window opposite the reception desk. Yet, the door wasn't as heavy as it used to be, and the distance across the room to the window was shorter, and the chair was lower, but, strangest of all, she was seized by an overwhelming conviction that she herself was not the same person who had been here before.

For a giddy instant she was whirled about by the thought, "Maybe they really have been a dream, these whole two years. Maybe I've come to the end of it, back at the beginning where I started, and I really am on the verge of waking up and discovering there never was a Dr. Kruger or an office or any of the things that happened."

Someone was calling her, someone far off, yet nearby. It dawned on her slowly that it was her father, saying, "Cathy! Come out of the fog. The nurse is speaking to you."

"Dr. Kruger is ready to see you," the nurse repeated, amused. She slipped a warm, slim hand into Cathy's. "If you want to leave your dog out here with your father, I'll take you in."

Cathy followed obediently, and again a pattern of familiar strangeness met her. There was Dr. Kruger's routine mumbled greeting, his routine grunts as he seated her at the big machine where she fitted her face into the well-remembered chin and forehead rest, the routine shift of seats to the dentist's chair in the center of the room, the routine requests to "Look up, please," "Look down, please," and "Look straight ahead, please." What was anything but routine, especially for him, were his attempts to make conversation. "That's a beautiful dog you have there. What is his name?" "Where are you going to school this year?" "How is the work there? Pretty hard?" "How did you do on your exams?" Most startling, though, was the comment, "Do you know, I didn't recognize you when I glanced in the reception room? You must have been busy this year, growing up."

Before she could produce a suitable reply, he added, "Look straight ahead once more, please. What can you see?"

She stared intently into space. "Nothing."

"And now?" His sleeve rustled as he moved his hand.

She squinted more earnestly and drew in a breath. "Nothing."

"And here?"

Was that a glimmer of light to her left? She pressed her utmost strength into the effort to see it. Moisture gathered on her lashes from the strain, and she had to wink. In the second her eyes were shut, the pin prick of light did not flicker. It remained as stationary as her mental images of Dr. Kruger and of his inner office— as stationary as her other mental images.

"No," she said, in a voice that got stuck a fraction above a whisper. "Nothing."

Dr. Kruger laid down the instrument he was using, which experience told her was his thin, doctor's flashlight. The click of it against the metal of the instrument table was like the click of something inside her being closed.

"How do your eyes feel?" he asked. "Do they pain you ever? They don't have any soreness, do they? Or aches, or extra sensitiveness that bother you?"

She shook her head. The closed place was in her throat, where her voice should be.

"Fine! Very good," he said, with what for Dr. Kruger was great heartiness. "I guess we couldn't reasonably ask for much more, since you're doing so well in everything these days." He got to his feet and offered his hand to help her from the chair. "Just keep up the good work, and don't let anybody steal that handsome dog from you."

It was now or never if the vital, basic question was to be asked, but Cathy did not ask it. The answer was hers already in that short, absolute statement that sealed her ears to everything else as she left the office with her father: "We couldn't reasonably ask for much more."

Much more than she had now, was what he meant. She couldn't reasonably ask for much more than nothing.

Cathy was grateful to her father for not wanting to talk on the drive home. Tears would be the ultimate defeat, but for a while it was the most she could do to control her mouth from quivering. She had been aware for a long time now that the specks and spots of light that remained to her after the operation were gradually disappearing, but she had never admitted it consciously, even to herself, and she had not given up hope. It was giving up hope that was agonizing, watching helplessly as it was crushed to death under the smothering weight of that awful word *Forever*. Why couldn't Dr. Kruger have spared her this by telling her the truth there in the hospital, eighteen months ago? He must have been fairly certain of what was to come. Why did he have to be such a coward?

Yet, how would she have lived through those eighteen months without hope? And if she had been so convinced herself that she was likely to be able to see tomorrow, why had she gone through all the stress and struggle of getting Trudy?

She leaned down to stroke the broad head lying at her feet. Trudy, curled up neatly beneath the dashboard, lifted her muzzle and rested her chin on Cathy's knee.

"You are a beauty," Cathy murmured. "And to think that this time last year I was locked up in Burton, and didn't know you existed."

A picture of Burton—its dark, narrow halls, its dingy, unpolished stairways, its drab, blank walls—rose up in her mind as sharply as a photograph. Her mind was in the habit of playing tricks like that on her, translating the messages of her ears and fingers and nose into such visual details that, too often, she caught herself describing to somebody rooms and landscapes she had not actually seen. Unless she bumped her head on a half-open door or unless a person like Joan insisted on reminding her, she was seldom truly conscious that her eyes were not functioning. She was generally too busy thinking of other things.

It flashed on her suddenly, as the car pulled away from a stop sign, that it was when she did get to thinking of herself as blind, when she let her confidence be shaken and her self-respect be trampled down by the jealous Joans and Francies, the bullying Miss Creels and the weak and selfish Petes she met, that was when she wound up bruised and miserable. She would have to ignore them from now on, would have to be bigger than their pettiness and forge ahead to her goals in spite of them. She would have to learn to understand people better, the fine ones and the warped, and to judge them all aright. Perhaps she should make that a second small candle to keep burning beside the first: to know and consider the other person before she worried about herself.

"I think I'll write to Daisy tonight," she said, leaning back against the seat. "I haven't done it since September."

"Not getting homesick for Burton, are you?" her father teased.

"Never!" Cathy screwed her face into a grimace and shuddered. "But Daisy was my best friend, and she's pretty lonely there. And Burton's the worst spot on earth, even if you aren't lonesome."

"Then I take it you won't object if I send Miss Creel a copy of your report card?" There was a smile in his voice, but he was slowing the car and swinging in toward the curb before she had time to answer. "I'm letting you off here at the corner of our block. I have a business call still to make this afternoon, and I'm close to being late. You can tell your mother I expect to be home early for supper, though."

Cathy was on the sidewalk, listening to the departing hum of his motor, when it occurred to her that she had forgotten to mention her appointment to the *Times*. Well, it would be a grand surprise to spring on everyone at once at the supper table.

There were no more flakes in the air, but the new snow crunched beneath her boots and squeaked under Trudy's paws as they started homeward. Cathy's skin tingled in the cold, clean air, and she sniffed a trace of wood smoke mingled with the freshness. Perhaps there was a hot, crackling fire awaiting her in the living room fireplace. And perhaps forever wasn't so devastating if you just took it a day or an hour or a minute at a time.

"Hey, Cathy!" burst Mark's unmistakable bawl from the far end of the block. "Hurry it up. There's a phone call for you."

"Who is it?" she called, quickening her steps.

"A guy named Steve. It's important, he says. He's going to call back in fifteen minutes."

Cathy's heart did a double flip. The hope she had thought eternally dead popped up from its grave clothes, green and new and alive as spring. Maybe it wasn't quite the same as the sprig she thought she had buried, but its roots were deep in the right place and its leaves were just as glossy. And anyway, she didn't have time to stop and examine it.

"Come on, Trudy," she said, giving the harness a shake. "Let's go!"

And together, they broke into a run.

ABOUT THE AUTHOR

BEVERLY BUTLER lost her sight at the same age as Cathy in *Light a Single Candle*. Miss Butler learned to read and write Braille and under the guidance of her dog, Sister, she finished high school and graduated *cum laude* from Mount Mary College. She was awarded a Woodrow Wilson Fellowship and received her M.A. degree from Marquette University in 1961. Miss Butler now lives in Milwaukee and teaches writing courses at Mount Mary. *Gift of Gold*, the sequel to *Light a Single Candle*, is also in an Archway Paperback edition.